FOR THOSE ABOUT TO READ, WE SALUTE YOU!

About the Spartapuss series...

'Cattastic' – London Even Standard

'Non-stop adventure... Spartapuss serves notice that cattitude rules!' – I Love Cats (USA)

'It's Rome AD36 and the mighty Feline Empire rules the world. This is the diary of slave cat Spartapuss, who finds himself imprisoned and sent off to gladiator school to learn how to fight, for fight he must if he wants to win his freedom. Packed with more catty puns than you ever thought pawsible, this witty Roman romp is history with cattitude.' – Scholastic Junior Magazine

'Spartapuss makes history fun instead of dull...For people who don't like history (like me), this book might change their minds.' – Shruti Patel, aged 10

'I really enjoyed this book and I liked the fact that it was written as if it was Spartapuss's diary. My favourite character was Russell (a crow!!!) Spartapuss's friend. I would recommend this book for ages 10+ especially if you enjoy books with a twist and a sense of humour.'
– Sam (11-year-old Young Archaeologist member from York)

'A truly hilarious story... One of the UK's brightest new authors.' ... 'A must read for children and cat lovers'.

'...a unique couple of books that have really caught the imagination of the public here... clearly something special.'

'Catligula's reign, a time when cats ruled Rome, was short if bloody, a story told by freedcat Spartapuss, employed as a scribe by Catligula, whose life was saved by Spartapuss. The Emperor is mad, poisoning those he believes to be his enemies and making his pet, Rattus Rattus, a member of the Senate. The Spraetorian Guard are determined to end his reign before Catligula ruins the empire.

Based loosely upon the writings of classical historians, Catligula is the second in a series that re-tells the scandals of the early Caesars in an accessible form, inevitably reminiscent of Robert Graves' *I, Claudius*. The jokes lie mainly in the names – the Greeks become Squeaks – but the descriptions of life in classical Rome are good, particularly the set piece in the Arena, when Catligula plays himself in what must have been an embarrassing display to even his sycophantic feline audience.

Readers who know the original stories will enjoy the fun, and those who don't know the history may be enticed to look more closely at the Roman stories.'

'This is too good to be left just as a children's book! Extremely funny and brilliantly written. Robin Price has taken the events of Roman history focusing around the time of Emperors Tiberious, Caligula and Claudius and turned it into something fascinating.'
— Monsters and Critics.com

'Two paws up! A stylish, witty and thoroughly engaging tale that will captivate young and old readers alike.'
— Tanuja Desai Hidier, author of 'Born Confused'
(Winner of the London Writer's Award for Fiction 2001)

'I would recommend them... Thrillers that you can't put down 'til you've read the whole thing.'
— Fiona Murray (reader reviewer) The Journal of Classics Teaching

BOUDICAT

ROBIN PRICE

MOGZILLA

BOUDICAT

First published by Mogzilla in 2008

Paperback edition:
ISBN 13: 9781906132019

Hardback edition:
ISBN 13: 9781906132002

www.mogzilla.co.uk

Printed in Malta

The author would like to thank the following
people for all of their help and encouragement:

Mum and Dad, Michele, Peter, Hayley, The Chariot, Christina, Sam, Phil, Rupert, Nick, Sinc, Andrew, Bev, Les, Kirsty, Twiz, Ed, Tanuja, Jon, Olivia, Nicole and Nicholas R.

For Heather, Josh & Scarlet...

THE TALE SO FAR...

Boudicat is the fourth book in the SPARTAPUSS series. You don't need to have read the other three titles to enjoy Boudicat. It is set in Roman times in a world ruled entirely by cats, where humans have never existed.

In I AM SPARTAPUSS, the first book in the series, SPARTAPUSS is comfortable managing Spatopia, Rome's finest Bath and Spa. He is a loyal servant to his master CLAWDIUS – a cat of the Imperial Family.

But Fortune has other plans for him. There is a nasty incident in the vomitorium. It causes offence to 'CATLIGULA' the would-be heir to the throne. SPARTAPUSS is thrown into prison, only to be released into gladiator training school. At the end of his training, he is given a golden coin by his teacher TEFNUT. He fights at the Games and is freed by CATLIGULA. Shortly afterwards, SPARTAPUSS rescues CATLIGULA from a chariot crash.

CATLIGULA is the second book in the series. When CATLIGULA becomes Emperor, his madness brings Rome to within a whisker of disaster. He poisons those he believes are his enemies and makes his pet RATTUS RATTUS a senator. The SPRAETORIAN GUARD plot to get rid of him and need SPARTAPUSS to help. SPARTAPUSS agrees but at the last minute changes his mind and helps CATLIGULA to escape. He convinces the Emperor that he is needed to perform a play. During the performance, the Arena is flooded in mysterious circumstances and CATLIGULA is lost. The Emperor's PURRMANIAN BODYGUARDS go on the rampage, looking for revenge for the death of their master. They find CLAWDIUS (CATLIGULA's uncle) hiding on top of a cupboard. On SPARTAPUSS'S suggestion, they pronounce that CLAWDIUS is Emperor of the Known World.

In DIE CLAWDIUS, the third book in the series, CLAWDIUS decides to invade The Land of the Kitons. SPARTAPUSS finds himself rounded up and forced aboard the first ship in the invasion fleet. He joins the landing party that sets out to search for the Kiton Army. Captured by two warriors, he escapes into the woods, where he meets FURG, a young Kiton studying to become a MEWID. After joining her at MEWID school, Spartapuss realizes he must choose between his new friends and the Emperor. Angry at the Roman invaders, FURG storms off to join the rebel army. SPARTAPUSS decides stay and look for her.

In BOUDICAT, the fourth book in the series, eighteen years have passed since the Invasion, and SPARTAPUSS, has grown rich, (like many Roman settlers).

DRAMATIS PAWSONAE

Who's who!

From the deserts of Fleagypt to the forests of Purrmania, The Feline Empire rules the known world.

As Spartapuss takes up his diary again in AD 61, The Land of the Kitons has been under Roman rule for nearly eighteen years.

The Romans:

Nero – Young Emperor of Rome, a terrible singer.
Governor Mewtonius – rules The Land of the Kitons on behalf of the Emperor.
The Procurator – collects taxes for the Emperor.

The Kitons:

King Praws – Old King of the Micini
Boudicat – Queen of the Micini tribe
Mane and Curl – two warriors of the Micini tribe

The Boar Horse – a mythical beast, pictured on the coins of the Micini tribe

Find out more at *www.mogzilla.co.uk*

MEWNONIUS XXVIII

June 28th

A Bill and a Will

This is the diary of Spartapuss. I am finding it hard to get started this time, as I have not taken pen to paw for many long years.

Why did I stop writing? Many summers ago I saved an old cleaner from a burning house. She was beating at the flames with a big brush, when I dragged her out to a safe place. She thanked me and promised to do me a favour if I bought her a fowl dinner. Luckily, there are very many places where you can get a fowl dinner here in The Land of the Kitons. We Romans say that it is the land nearest to The Land of the Dead. This shows in their food. They have two different 'schools' of cooking dinner here: boil it to mush or burn it to ash. At any rate, I took the old cleaner to a roast bird place near my house. There are many of these roasting shops in the east of the town of Londump. The pigeons of East Londump have become the fastest flappers in the whole of the Feline Empire. They have to move fast to escape the roasting tins of the locals.

Well, we soon got our whiskers into our bowls and began to strip the blackened meat off the bones. Suddenly, the old cleaner popped out a gnarled claw and flipped my bowl up. High up in the air it sailed,

as high as Apawllo's chariot. Then it fell to the floor
with a clatter.

"For Peus, sake!" I said. "I'm paying good money
for that bird! I'll have it if you don't want it."

Shaking and hissing, the old cleaner sprang up onto
the table and clawed at my pigeon bones like a wolf in
winter. Now, I took her for a cleaner because she had
this great big brush made of twigs. She would not let
it out of her sight and clung to it, even as I dragged
her out of the flames. I know something of brushes, as
I am now in the brush trade myself. This one was on
a great long stick, like our brooms but rougher with
big bristles.

This cleaner might also have what the locals call
'the gift'. For it is said that there are many witches
in this strange land. Witches often tell the future by
'reading the bones'. In fact, bones are a popular read
in this island, where books are rare as a rainless
summer.

The old tabby looked at the bones and then at me,
and then up to the sky. She carried on like this for a
long time. So long that I nearly asked the innkeeper for
separate bills. At last, she looked at me and told me to
listen very carefully. She called me to come close.

"You've been unlucky," she hissed. "Cursed,
even."

"I wouldn't go that far," I replied. Although it is true
that I have had some unlucky spins from Fortune.

"Silence!" she spat. "I've seen the truth, so listen if

you want to hear it."

In a whisper, she told me that the reason was my writing.

"It is an unlucky business, especially for the likes of you," she hissed. "But, there is hope."

She said that if I promised not to write a single word for the next twelve summers, I would soon get richer. I could be as rich as honey mouse cake, even. But only if took her advice and left my pen in its ink pot.

Now, this tabby was a stranger, with a flea problem and a touch of 'crab coat', a common disease of the skin in this land where they are strangers to the bath house, for they cannot stand the touch of water on their coat. This can cause many diseases of the skin. Perhaps this why she carried such a big brush? I have mentioned that already, have I not? I grow old, and it is said that the old are likely to repeat themselves.

At any rate, like the great heroes in the stories of old, I decided to do exactly as this old tabby said. That very day, I put down my pen and I have not written a single word since.

That must have been twelve summers ago at the least, although my memory is not what it was when I was younger, I am told. However, I cannot be sure how good it was then, for I cannot remember.

At any rate, the Goddess Fortune has smiled on me ever since that day. For I got into the grooming business. Who would have thought that Roman-style combs and silver backed brushes would have become so popular in this wild and bathless land? And who would have thought that I, Spartapuss, a freed slave, would own houses in his own name. I now have three fine houses, if you count my Londump loft as a house. I also have a share in a field in the town of Ferulanium. The builder who sold it to me swore by Purlin's Sword that it would make someone rich. He did not say who, exactly, but I am sure that it will be me. For my end of the field is full of the most important thing you need to build houses in this land: pure mud.

So reader, I can promise that this new diary, unlike my others, will not be full of gladiators or the terrors of the arena; of dread battles and unfortunate disasters here in Land of the Kitons; of evil creatures and who are ready to tear me apart in every sentence! We will have no chapters where cruel Gods play with me - like a toy mouse on a string. There will be absolutely none of that sort of thing. Now I am a land owner and respectable and I have promised my wife that all of that is in the past. Also, I promise to do none of that Squeak style of flowery writing that is popular back in Rome these days. I have read menus in this land that are funnier than those so called comic poets, Sprayto and the rest. It is a shame that they have all been dead for so many years, as they could have taken up tragedy. My writing is really tragic, according to my wife, who has started to read at least half of it. So perhaps I could have given old Sprayto a few tips.

Finally, an apology. I must now beg your pardon in advance if my writing is hard to make out. As I have said, I've written nothing since that day in the chicken shop. Rather than writing my name, I usually make my mark instead. This can be messy, to say nothing of the smell. So, if a shopkeeper wants it on paper, I dip a claw into the ink and make the sign of an X, in the place where the name of Spartapuss should be. If you stick with my scribbling, you'll soon get the hang of it. I may even get some poor scribe to lay it out neatly for me one day.

MEWNONIUS XXIX

June 29th

I woke up this morning in pain. The whiskers on the right side of my face were giving me the old trouble again. Hearing noises outside, I called for Leasha but there was no answer. After five minutes of shouting like a crow, I remembered that all of our servants are away. So I had to drag myself from my warm basket to find out what was going on.

After some time spent scratching at the lock, I got the gate open. Wolves can be a problem here, as is the dog next door. It is an ex-chariot dog. A very angry thing. It has retired from racing and taken up a new hobby: digging into our walls. Our beautiful home is an exact copy of a Roman villa. It is a very happy place to live, especially as it has been going up in value for each of the eighteen years since it was built. I am sure that this will carry on. Graftpuss, the builder, insisted on using 'local materials' for our villa. The result was our beautiful family home. It is a home of the finest quality. A villa made of mud is not typical for the town of Camolud and it did cause a small stir with the neighbors. Some of them have taken to throwing mud balls at our walls. This has now become something of a tradition - passed on from father to son. Perhaps the only problem is that a mud mansion is easily damaged. Especially by the retired terror next door. So on my way to my gate, I took a bag of apples to throw at the beast.

I soon found myself looking out upon a typical summer morning. That is to say it was grey, damp and cold enough to freeze the spinners off a marsh spider. And they have the biggest spinners of all the spiders in this dark island, it is said.

How I remember the crisp mornings of my carefree kitten days in Rome! They usually had me slaving at some task before sun up. But at least in Rome the sun shines when it comes out. Not like the sun over here in this island - which burns low, like a lamp with cheap oil.

After a bit of a poke around my courtyard, I found nothing. No wolf prints. No sign of next door's terrible hound. I was closing the gate when I spotted that the messenger had come. Rather than leaving my messages neatly in the box provided, he'd flung them into the yard. They landed right in the middle of my mud mosaic. All the lamps in my study are out of oil so I took the message into the kitchen to open. I could not believe what I read.

Dear Ginger One,

Happy Birthday!

We hope you enjoyed your birthday party. Here is your bill.

Yours,

DORPUSS

Keeper of The Oar Orse Inn

P.S. PLEASE PAY YOUR BILL, IF YOU VALUE YOUR TEETH!

MEWNONIUS XXX

June 30th

Writer's Block

I am still smarting from reading the bill. There is no way that I can afford to spend that much on a party. The food was cold and the musicians were terrible, as is traditional here in the land of the Kitons. As my wife and the servants are away, I must go myself to the inn and complain. I am getting back into the habit of writing now. As I said, I have not picked up a pen for twelve years long years. It all started when I met an old tabby.... Oh - I have told that part of the tale already, haven't I? Well it is true that during these years, which my wife calls my golden age, I have done no writing at all. However, I did have a large block made out of oak so that I can carve letters and words, if the mood takes me. The old tabby said nothing about carving you see, so I got around it with this wooden block. Having a writer's block is lovely. Every writer should get one.

CATILIS I

July 1st

Today I went to the inn, and told the innkeeper that he is a thief. By the time I learned that I was in the wrong inn, a large crowd had gathered. They would not let me out until I had bought cream-bowls for all. The locals here like talking to strangers but are not so good at listening. I learned that the greens are likely to win at the chariot racing (which I do not follow). I learned that this year's summer festival was good - and the statues burned up very nicely, all pinky orange. This should make for a good harvest. The talk of the room was the sad death of Old King Praws. He was a wise ruler, for a Micini at least, it is said. Not everyone in the inn was friendly. I am sorry to say that we Romans are not very well liked across this land. Why we are hated so much I cannot say. My wife says it is because Rome invaded this land and now the Emperor owns the best bits of it. She may be right, so I have decided to be very careful when talking about this king or that tribe. Although the locals talk of very little else, except the weather and the chariots. At last, I found a useful bit of information. It is *The Oar Orse* inn in Gnaw-Itch that I want.

CATILIS IV

July 4th

The weather is so bad that I have decided not to go looking for mysterious inns. I cannot send a servant. They have all gone. There is no one to do things for me anymore. My son is away in Rome, visiting a festival. "Please father! It is a once in a lifetime trip," he pleaded. "It had better be," I said, when I heard what it would cost. "When I was your age, all the festivals were free." "Please father!" The Emperor himself will be playing," he purred. Rome's latest Emperor has been in power for seven years now since poor Clawdius died. Clawdius was poisoned by the paw of his own wife as he lay on the Cushioned Throne, it is said. She knew he could never resist a sardine stuffed with mushrooms. Young Clawdius Mewsus Purrmanicus, or 'Nero' as he likes to be called, fancies himself as a great artist. He loves acting and singing, and he puts on festivals each year where the mob can even take part in singing competitions. It is my son's dream that he will win one of these competitions and become known as the creamy voice from the Land of the Kitons. It is good to have dreams that can come true easily. This is a land of howlers where they cannot carry a tune in a bucket. My son also tells me that there was talk of holding a music festival here. That is a most stupid idea. What fool would want to put on a festival of music in a muddy field? At last I gave in and agreed to let my son go to Rome for the festival. On hearing this, he leapt up for joy and purred like a windmill. He stopped purring when he heard that his mother was going, to make sure he doesn't not get into trouble. For a warrior, she is a dreadful worrier.

CATILIS V

July 5th

Trouble in Gnaw-Itch

This morning I got up before crow's caw and set out on the road to the town of Gnaw-Itch. At last, I found the inn. Behind the counter I found the innkeeper, who was almost as fat as one of his own milk-barrels. He scratched and then licked his paws in a way that cannot be healthy, especially when serving cold meats. "Is this *The Oar Orse Inn?*" I asked, wanting to make sure I had got the right place. The whole room began to shake with laughter. I later learned that it was *The Boar Horse Inn*. The landlord's writing was little better than scribble. My own writing is little better. *The Boar Horse* is a very common name for an inn in the Gnaw-itch area, as this beast is the symbol of The Micini tribe. They paint pictures of it on their shields and battle flags. This is said to be an island of animal lovers, and they are especially found of deadly ones.

"Listen fellow," I said, waving the bill under the innkeeper's nose. "You've charged me for thirteen courses of food when I swear I only saw six. Your snails were rotting in their shells and your cream bowls were only half full. And what is this extra charge for?"

The landlord raised himself to his full height and let out a low hiss.

"Music," he replied, reading the bill.

"Music?" I hissed, "The noise those rag-tails made was awful. I've heard cart accidents that are easier on the ear."

Without another word, the landlord leapt over the bar and held me by the throat. Then he caught me in a place which hurt even more - my wallet. He grabbed it from my closed paw and emptied it onto the table. Out fell my last aurus. It didn't glitter, but the innkeeper knew the coin was pure gold.

"That'll do nicely, sir," he said with a grin, letting go of my throat. Disappearing under the counter, he came back with a leather bag. On opening it - he gave me four small silver coins. I examined each of these carefully for holes or cuts, as there is a lot of bad money about.

"What type of coins are these?" I asked uneasily.

"There's nothing wrong with them," he said. "That's a Boar Horse sir – a Micini coin."

"It doesn't look much like a boar," I said, cringing at the fantastically ugly animal on the front.

"It don't look much like a horse either," laughed the landlord. "It bites like a good 'un though."

I am not at all sure what he meant by this. I suppose I should have thanked the goddess Fortune for leaving the inn with any change at all. I will thank her properly tonight, in my prayers. It is important that the Goddess is in a good mood because tomorrow, I must attend an important event. A windfall would do me very nicely, as I've had lots of expenses. I wonder if it's worth a little sacrifice? I cannot remember where my wife keeps the wood for the alter.

CATILIS VI

July 6th

How I wish my dear wife was here - rather than running around enjoying herself in Rome. I have set off for the centre of Gnaw-Itch and I am certain that they have nothing in that town to compare with the sights of Rome, like our stunning *Temple of Mewpiter*, or the magnificent *Paw's Field* where our army does its training. There is also a *Paw's Field* in Gnaw-Itch, but it is full of a vegetable they call mangelwurzels, as it is a field belonging to a local farmer called Paws.

I am going to the town on foot as there is no servant to take me by chariot. This will save money, as they have just extended the zone of the chariot charge. Old King Praws, the King of the Micini, died last week and I am to attend the reading of his will. It is very likely that members of his family and 'close friends' will be all over his silver and jewelry like ants on a sweet plate. It is said that he had the biggest collection of torcs in the whole of the land. My wife was a distant relative of the king and there is a little hope that he might have remembered her in his will.

CATILIS VII

July 7th

Ill Will

My paw shakes as I write these words. I have just had a lucky escape at the reading of the old King's will. I am glad to be alive and writing this, although many in that hall would not say the same. The dead do not write, which is a shame because they probably have the time for it. I shall now try to relax in my basket, as I tell what happened to me on this terrible day.

Gnaw-itch is said to be an ugly town, so when I arrived at the gates I was surprised to find that they have been decorated - with the heads of some local criminals. A sign read:

WE STRING STEALERS UP!

There was little to see except some rotting fur and white bones nailed to a post. Gnaw-itch is a town that is not best known for its friendliness. I will not bore you with the details of how I found the hall for the reading of the King's will. However, I took many wrong turns and arrived late. It was a large hall but packed to bursting with the King's family and many other hangers on, all hoping to make a profit. It was like a locust reunion on Swarming Day. So packed was it in the hall that I couldn't see what was going on. I was afraid it would be like this. Luckily, I'd dressed in my Roman clothes so that I could get a seat in the Roman VIP area. As I made my way through the crush, the crowd began to boil and spit like a new cauldron.

"Half!" shrieked a tatty old female, with a nose like a rotten prune. She poked a claw in my direction, to help to make her point. I smiled and carried on towards the Roman seats.

"Half!" "Half!" "Half!" soon others took up the shout.

"Excuse me," I said to the back of a tall fellow in front. He spun to face me.

"What do you want, Roman?" he hissed.

"Nothing," I muttered, moving aside. Further on, I saw a friendlier looking face and decided to find out what was happening.

"I am having trouble seeing. Have they started reading out the will?"

"Aye. The king wants everything split in half," said the stranger.

"Really!" I exclaimed. "That is a shame. Rotten luck for whoever gets his boats and his battle chariot. Half a boat wouldn't be much good on the water."

The tall one glared at me, tilting his head to one side.

"He means, they want to split the whole kingdom

up in half," sniffed a nasty piece of work at his side.

"Queen Boudicat is only going to get half her kingdom. It's a disgrace!" added another. There were cries and shouts of "Shame!" and "Death to the Snail Eaters" from all around. For some reason the Kitons cannot understand the Roman's love of the snail. Perhaps it is because the herb garlic cannot be found in this land of dark stews.

"So who will get the other half?" I asked, playing for time.

"Who do you think? Your cursed Emperor of course," said the tall one with a hiss. "May mighty Woool chop off his…"

"I see. Many thanks friends." I replied. Deciding not to ask him the way to the Roman VIP seats, I pushed my way through the crowd to the left. This was most unusual. The old King had left half of everything to Rome. This hall was no place for a stranger in Roman clothes! At last I caught sight of the VIP seats. They were empty! I was about to try to slip off when I felt a claw at my throat. Twisting free, I leapt onto a large urn and faced my attacker.

"We don't like Romans, in these parts," he said, in a voice as crabby as the local apples.

"Don't you?" I said. "I thought the Micini were always the friends of Rome."

"We're not the Micini – we're the Trinos," spat another. He was a huge ginger lump with claws like butcher's hooks. His ragged ears marked him as a scrapper. As for his tribe, well I can never remember all of the tribes in this war-like land – for they are as plentiful as the slugs in springtime. Yet I was sure that I'd heard of the Trinos somewhere before.

"Haven't the Trinos always been the friends of Rome as well?" I said, risking a smile.

"No!" hissed my attacker, bristling with rage.

"Not since you Romans took the town of Camolud from us," said an old fellow at his side.

"Ah? Those Trinos," I said, remembering the sad story of that unlucky tribe.

"Your cursed Caesar turned it into a colony for his old soldiers," said the old one. "Now the Romans are building mansions there on our lands. Mansions made of mud! While we live in huts."

"Think yourself lucky," said another, "our huts don't even have roofs on them."

Now, in fact they were wrong. It wasn't Caesar who turned them out, it was Patlius Strocula. These Kitons will call anything in a chariot 'Caesar'. It's one of the only Roman words they know. I myself am sometimes called Caesar at the local inns and even by my own servants. No matter how many times I correct them, they cannot seem to remember my name. But I decided to let this mistake pass, for I felt that this was not the time to try to win an argument.

"Rome be cursed!" spat the old Trino. "You want to take away our weapons and make us into mice!"

By now a large part of the crowd had turned to watch

the argument. There was an long and brooding silence, so I decided that I had to say something.

"Come on. The old Emperor Clawdius told Patlius off for that – didn't he? You can still carry your weapons, can't you?" At once each Kiton in the crowd took out his or her weapon and waved it at me. I saw axes, blades and the big bone-crushing broadswords that the Kittish warriors like so much. There were also some silver sickles - so I guessed that there were a few Mewids in the hall. Do not get me started on the topic of Mewids. I tried to help them once. But after what they did to my poor wife, I will have nothing more to do with them. She was made one of *The Forgotten*, as they call those who leave their Sacred Order. There is no time for a full tale now, but let it be known that I have a horror of the Mewid's curved blades. I cannot help but wonder if their pretty silver sickles had been cutting more than mistletoe and holly.

All Talk

As I looked out across that hall, I wondered how the crowd had come to hate me. My wife would never have let me go out into the town wearing Roman clothing! I can often pass for a member of the Catre tribe – on account of my ginger coat. But I cannot speak their language, although my wife has tried to teach me. She is in Rome, keeping our son out of trouble. But what of her poor husband? Seeing that spitting, seething crowd, I knew I would be lucky to make it out of the room with my ginger coat still on my back.

"Friends," I shouted, "wait! What did The Queen say when she heard the terrible news that she will only get her noble paws on half of the kingdom?" The crowd fell silent as stones. Then I heard myself saying: "I see Mewids amongst you. Ask them what the Queen wants us to do about this terrible wrong? What are the Queen's orders?'

"What does Queen Boudicat say?" came a shout.

"We haven't told her yet," said an embarrassed figure in a white robe.

"The messengers are on strike again," moaned a second Mewid.

"Just wait till Queen Boudicat finds out," called a voice from the back. "Her wrath will be like a mighty hammer falling from the sky. Her fur will bristle and she'll start to spit – then she will unsheathe her claws and begin to tear. And whoever is in that room will wish they were sleeping in the cold bog, next to her dead husband – rather than live to feel her rage."

"I wouldn't like to be there when she finds out," I agreed. Now, I had no idea what was coming next, but perhaps I should have guessed it. Fortune was about to spin me another wrong one. For the vile fellow who had put his claws on me had a smile on his face!

"Send the Roman. Send the Roman to tell the Queen!" he cried. And the whole crowd took up the chant.

CATILIS IX

July 9th

Shoot the Messengers

So here I am on the road again. I escaped from the hall alive. But I agreed to take the bad news to Queen Boudicat. I had no choice. Well – that is not quite true – I was given a choice: deliver the message – or stand trial by the 'Old Ways' of the Mewids. Rather than hang around till the next full moon for the sickle to fall, I decided to become a messenger. It is three days journey to the Queen's lands and I fear that it will be a long walk on short rations, with a bitter end. But a lucky spin from the goddess Fortune! Ahead of us on the road I have seen the flag of an Imperial Envoy. If we march hard, we may catch them up and make camp with him tonight. How marvellous it will be to hear the news from Rome the noble language of Catin. One grows tired of howling in Kittish all day long. Perhaps he will invite me to dinner? I hope there are no snails on the menu as I have gone off them since my party.

CATILIS X

July 10th

Last night I went to meet The Imperial Envoy. I was thrown out of his tent by two auxiliaries.

Apparently, he does not eat with 'the locals'. I wonder if it is for fear of poisoning or for obvious reasons of taste?

CATILIS XIII
July 13th

At last we drew near to Queen Boudicat's palace. I have only met the Queen once and that went badly. I cannot imagine what in Paws name she will do when she hears the bad news about her lands. The Envoy is camped at the gates too. I wonder if he is also here to bring her news. Whatever it is, it cannot be worse than what I have to tell her.

CATILIS XIV
July 14th

A Royal Shedding

At the gates of the Queen's Home, I met up with The Imperial Envoy - and his party. 'Party' is the wrong word for that crew - a couple of rough look-ing Scenturians and a cohort of Auxiliaries - from Hisspania by the look of them. They pushed in front of me, but were made to wait at the gate. Only the Envoy, the two Scenturians and I were allowed to pass through the Royal gate.

It is said that the Royal Home of Queen Boudicat

and old King Praws is very impressive. It is said, but whoever says that has only seen it from the outside. As I padded through the great oak gates, the colour of the walls put me in mind of a hunting accident.

"It cannot be easy being a Royal. When they are not waging bloody war, they do a lot of good work," I said. The Envoy did not answer, he just sniffed and turned his nose up. It is true that the smell of the horses was most powerful. As we were led towards the great hall, I saw where the smell was coming from. It was a horse inside the villa! To the Micini, the Horse is a sacred animal. In Rome they are considered unlucky. The only mysterious power they have is the power to take money from fools. We Romans prefer to use reliable dogs to pull both chariots and carts. Now the smell of horse is very strong. Once it gets into your wall hangings - you simply cannot get rid of it. But when it is mixed with the smell of pig, it is almost unbearable. And soon it became clear that the old King was a pig lover too. For around the next corner, we came face to face with an enormous wild pig. I shall not forget the look of horror on the face of The Envoy when this bristling beast grunted at him. He was so shocked that he began to shed his summer coat!

GREAT MANE
At last I reached the door that lead to The Great Hall. It was guarded by a couple of long-faced Kitons. They looked as if they'd missed breakfast two days in a row.

Their names were Mane and Curl. The first had long claws like meat knives – the other was also a big cat, although he looked like a kitten next to the other. I learned later that he took his name from his long tail that curled up as sharply as his mouth curled down.

"Summon Queen Boudicat immediately slaves!" demanded the Envoy, still coughing from the smell. One of the Kitons gave him a terrible look and unsheathed his claws. The Envoy was so surprised that he leapt behind a cushion, knocking over the pig's swill bucket.

"Er, I think these fellows are warriors, not slaves," I said. "I'm sure he didn't mean any offence." The first Kiton nodded, leaning back on his shovel. "Not that I've got anything against slaves," I added. "I was a slave myself, once." The one called Curl stopped dead in his tracks and gave me a strange look.

"Get up and stop grovelling Roman," ordered his friend. The Envoy now had his front paws in the pig's dinner. And pigs are not above licking their dinner off your paws.

"Call it off! Call it off now, in the name of Caesar Best and Greatest!" begged the Envoy, trembling with fear as he felt the animal's wet tongue on his feet.

"Stop whining Snail-eater. That one's only a baby!" laughed Curl. He gently gave the beast a prod with a long-handled stick that had seen a lot of use. Then he turned to me and smiled. "Come this way. Queen Boudicat will see you now."

TORC OF THE TOWN

As we entered into Queen Boudicat's hall I caught site of a surprisingly young-looking cat. She was feeding a little pig with scraps out of a silver bucket. Around her neck was a lovely silver collar, in the torc style. The width of the silver was amazing – it must have given her neck ache. It was dangling so low that it almost kissed the swill bucket. Her orange coat was sleek and it gleamed in the light from the high window.

"The queen is younger than I thought!" I said, taken by surprise.

"That's not the Queen – that's only one of her daughters," said Curl. "The rest of them will be off playing pull-the-tail-off-the-donkey somewhere."

Curl led us to the back of the Great Hall. Now pretty much any building with a roof in this land is called a 'Great Hall' but this one was a good size. Although it was strange having a wooden long hall in the middle of a Roman style Villa. Seated on a pile of cushions, sat a sleek cat with ink blue fur and eyes the colour of amber. Around her neck, she wore a silver torc collar like her daughter's, only thicker.

As we padded into the hall, a slave was giving her thick tail a good going over with a silver comb. Then, disaster! The comb snagged on a knot and there was a ripping noise. When a great clump of dark fur came out, the slave whimpered her apology, throwing herself on the ground. The mighty Queen of the Micini didn't even flinch. She simply laughed and picked up the comb. I thanked Peus that the comb was not one of mine, for we had a faulty batch of combs through from Fleagypt, with brittle teeth. The Queen told her slave to carry on grooming. I thanked Peus that warrior Queens have a low pain threshold.

THE WILD ONES

Queen Boudicat was surrounded by her warriors and her wild pigs. It was the filthiest, smelliest, most quarrelsome herd I have ever seen. And the pigs were little better. She beckoned us to come forward.

"Bow before me Romans," commanded the Queen, as her warriors began to roll about laughing. I think they may have been sniffing the bush that is called catnip, for they did not seem to be in their right minds. Now I like to get a good bit of grovelling in – low to the ground – nice and early in a situation like this. As I was saying to my son the other day, "A bit of grovelling can do no harm, especially with the ladies." However, the Envoy did not look happy about throwing himself in the dirt, in front of his soldiers. He gave only the slightest nod.

"Get up, Spartapuss, my sister's daughter's husband," said the Queen. "You are family. From the stupid side of the family perhaps. But you need not bow. Only this Roman has to lower his head before me. The warriors looked on in amazement. I thanked the Queen and smiled. But I could think only about the terrible rage that was to come when she heard my message. The Envoy bowed deeper for the second time and gave the Queen a scroll. Her warriors were a rough crew but they suddenly became very still and serious. For they knew that their Queen might turn on them at any moment. Boudicat stared at the scroll for some time, nodding and then shaking her head – looking both calm and wise. Then she dismissed the Envoy with a wave of the paw. He left the hall in a great hurry. Now, I was most surprised at this. For I knew that whatever the Emperor Nero had written on the scroll, it could not be good news for the Micini and Queen Boudicat. I knew this, not because I am a student of Kings, Queens and Emperors. I take little interest in the affairs of the great who rule us. No, I knew that Fortune had spun a wrong one, for the scroll had a special mark upon it. When I saw this terrible mark, it was all I could do not to turn tail and run. But before I could speak, the Queen rose and led me away from the gaze of her warriors, and gave the scroll to me. I stood before her in wonder and it was all I could do to stop my whiskers from twitching in fear. Curl, who had followed us, crept to my side.

"It is written in Catin," he said. "The Queen cannot read it, you must read it for her."

"This is the mark of the Procurator, whose job it is to collect all of the *taxes* in this land," I whispered, almost dropping the scroll as I spoke that dreaded name. Then I began to read.

Dear QUEEN BOUDICAT

I am writing to tell you that there has been a change in the way that the kingdom of the MICINI tribe has been divided. This change will affect your title of QUEEN of the MICINI
Due to a change in Roman law, kingdoms cannot be left in a will to any cat who was not born in Rome. The Emperor will take all of your lands, goods, treasure, slaves, food, clothing, art and anything else that may be carried off in a cart.

Yours

Clawrus,
Procurator, (Client Kingdoms division)

For the Senate and the People of Rome.

TAXES SHOULD NOT BE TAXING

On hearing this, Queen Boudicat let out a howl that shook the walls and rose up to the roof. She followed it, climbing the walls in her fury, until she had shaken the last crow from the rafters. Her warriors sprang up and the Queen grabbed her great horn and blew a lonely blast. At once, Curl appeared at her side - with her chariot pulled by two war dogs. Spitting with hate, she leapt into her chariot. And what I saw next, I know that some will find hard to believe. For she began to ride the chariot round and around the hall - whipping her followers into a fury. And then, she steered straight for the mud wall and burst right through it, chariot and all. Her warrior horde followed close behind, with her daughter at the front.

Now as I was watching all of this, I felt a tug at my collar. And I was scooped up and bundled into a chariot.

"Now the fun is about to start! Come on Spartapud, follow the Queen!" cried Curl. We plunged through down a rutted track after Boudicat's chariot.

"Hunting down the Envoy might not be a good idea," I said, for I guessed where we were going. "He was sent by the Emperor Nero himself."

"It wouldn't stop the Queen – even if he was sent by the Great Mother herself," laughed Curl.

By the time we caught up with Boudicat, it was too late to stop a disaster. She held a razor at the Envoy's throat. The fire of her rage had cooled. Now the Queen's words were bitter as a winter frost.

"Under Roman law I cannot have my husband's lands," she began. The Envoy had the sense not to interrupt Queen Boudicat. His body guards were all picked specially, the first was a Scenturian with a wild reputation and the second was a tough Auxiliary, fresh from battles in the forests of Maul. But the Queen swatted the first and the second escaped shaking like a stunned mouse.

"Rome would steal from me, and my children. Take everything that which was my husbands? That is mine? And you, Roman worm. You tell me you are not taxing?"

"It is just turn of phrase – your highness," whimpered the Envoy. "It means that tax does not have to be difficult."

"Very well. I will have your Procurator's hide, to warm the feet of my pigs. We'll see if he finds that taxing!"

So the Envoy was sent back, red-faced and howling, with a message for his master the Procurator, who was responsible for taxes. Boudicat had him painted and covered in feathers. As her warriors laughed at this sight, I stood in silence. For I know emperors better than queens. This insult cannot stand. A terrible chain of events has been set into motion. The Micini must now become a tribe of out-laws.

CATILIS XVI

July 16th

Forced to Feast

No one seems at all worried about what the Emperor will think when he finds out that Queen Boudicat has shaved his Envoy, beaten up his bodyguards and covered them with paint. Today the Micini warriors held a great feast, in their great hall. It was great. Staying here for the night has about as much appeal as a sinking ship for a rat. But I simply could not get away. Whenever I tried to make my excuses, another Micini warrior would step forward and challenge me. I have taken part in six flea-picking competitions so far today and I am quite sick of scratching. If I see another flea I will be visiting the Queen's vomitorium. That is if Queen Boudicat has a vomitorium. At my own party one of the guests was sick in the toilet - ignoring the vomitorium which we had built at great expense. Thankfully, I was spared one Micini tradition. Just as the coat-licking contest was about to begin, I was taken aside by Curl.

"Is it true you were a slave once," he asked. "How did you become free?"

"I won my freedom in the arena." I said.

"Where they fight to the death, in front of the crowd?" he said. I nodded. He stared at me, with the same amazement that he'd shown as we were waiting to enter the hall.

"Fighting to the death? That's kitten's play!" growled Mane, who had followed us out.

"You Romans know nothing of honour on the field of battle. Is freedom a prize, that it may be won in front of a mob?"

I turned towards the big Micini warrior. I have met his type many times. The sort who prickles with pride. The sort that boasts that he never goes looking for trouble, but always finds it. I knew that he'd be looking to pick a fight. So I was most careful not to give him an excuse. I was spared by the arrival of another Kiton noble, who had a bone to pick with Mane. It belonged to some large animal by the look of it. So I took my chance and slipped away.

SHOULD I STRAY, OR SHOULD I GO?
I am beginning to get a bad feeling about this place. I decided to leave whilst the warriors were asleep. Once a warrior has consumed a large amount of milk, flavoured with the catnip herb, he will become excited, and then sleepy. Many of the warriors fell asleep where they fell, and amongst the rest there was much jockeying for position to find the best sleeping places.

As Fortune wished it, no one wanted to be near the hole in the wall caused by the Queen's chariot – as rain is always likely in this land. At last, the warriors were snoring like pigs and the pigs were snoring like warriors. In the early light of dawn, I saw my chance and was about to slip through the hole. Then I felt a claw on my collar. A voice beside me said:

"Leaving so soon, I cannot allow it!" It was Queen Boudicat herself.

"I am sorry, great Queen. I would love to stay. But I must get back to Camulod."

The Queen's ears pricked up, and her bright eyes flashed with disapproval.

"Camulod?" she replied.

"Yes Queen. I promised my wife I'd look after our home. It's made of mud so its walls are weak."

The Queen of the Micini shook her head.

"You aren't going anywhere sister's daughter's husband. You are family – you are staying with me," she said firmly.

CATILIS XVII

July 17th

A Stinking Pit

Oh unhappy day. How I wish I had listened to my instinct! Her little voice gets lost in all the chatter of the day. I should have left this place yesterday - when I had the chance. It has come to this. The Micini have locked me in a cage made of wicker. They have swung this cage out over a pit. When I found the courage to look down, it was dark as a dungeon. It seems likely that I shall draw my last breath very soon. And it will not be a breath of fresh air either. The smell from the pit is enough to make a fishmonger choke. How is it that I came to such a pass? You will remember that last night I was trying to escape when I was stopped by Queen Boudicat herself. Mane and some of the others saw me talking to her. Well, this morning I woke up to a terrible panic. It seems that the Queen has vanished into thin air. Well, in truth the air in her hall was thick enough to chew on, after all of that feasting last night and the lack of proper ventilation. But at any rate - the warriors woke to find their Queen gone. Most Kitons are suspicious and it was not long before I found myself being blamed for the disappearing Queen.

"Friends, I don't know anything about this. For

only last night I spoke to the Queen and she was in fine health. I am sorry I cannot say more." It was Mane - who else, who stirred them all up against me.

"Down beast!" he cried, pressing my face into the dirt floor of the Great Hall. "Do not believe him my brothers. He is a spy sent by the Romans."

"No!" came a shout from the back. I could not believe it. Was someone about to speak up for me?

"He is not a spy," said a cold voice. "He is a magician, sent by the Romans."

"Or the flea-picking Trinos!" added another.

"Sent to make our Queen vanish, with dark magic," cried the first.

"Spy! Spy! Spy!" chanted one half of the hall.

"Sorcerer!" shrieked the others.

"Wait!" I begged, thinking that they would kill me right there on the spot. Mane now had his broadsword out and was licking the blade. But there was a cry for a trial. Then I was forced into this cage and swung out over the pit. That must have been a day ago and no one has said a word to me since. Perhaps I am to be left here forever? Or perhaps until Queen Boudicat returns.

CATILIS XVIII

July 18th

There is still no sniff of Queen Boudicat. Not that I could smell anything with the foul stench coming up from this pit. It is a nasty mixture of pig, horse and worse. Last night I could not sleep because of the snorting noises. But at last, a good spin from Fortune. In my cage this morning I found an apple. Now I do not like fruit as a rule. We Romans live on a diet of meat and fish, and will only eat grass and leaves when we are ill. I have not eaten since the day of the great feast so I am tempted to have a nibble.

CATILIS XIX

July 19th

Last night I had a strange dream, where I was flying. I awoke to find my cage pitching up and down like a boat in a storm. Now, I have tried not to think about it. But something lurks down in this pit. Last night it came up, roaring and tearing at the cage. I fear that each night will be my last.

CATILIS XX

July 20th

Strange Fruit

I am still here and another apple has been left in my cage. Sadly, the first apple was lost when the cage was shaken last night. It must have fallen out with all of that swinging. I have decided to stay awake all night - to find out who the Fruit Giver may be.

CATILIS XXI

July 21st

Apples for the Creature

Last night I was dozing when I felt the cage swinging once more. I feared that the beast was trying to shake me out of my bed again. I pretended to sleep but peaked out through my bars. Someone had swung me back towards the edge of the pit and was fiddling with the cage. I leapt up and cried out a curse. I shall not now record what I shouted. But if he had followed my instructions, it would have caused a scandal, even in the home of a barbarian.

"Be still. Keep your mouth shut if you value your hide," said a voice. It was Curl, with an apple in his paw.

"Thank you," I began. "I don't wish to sound ungrateful," but I am not really that fond of apples. A little fish or meat would be much more to my taste."

"They are not for you. They are for the creature. If it stirs again, hold the apple out of the side and let it fall."

"Thank Peus, I mean, thank The Great Mother for your help!" I said, not wanting to insult my helper. "I'm afraid that thing is more interested in eating me, than an apple."

Curl pushed his face up to mine - so that we were nose to nose through the bars. He spoke in a whispering half-hiss. "I do not mean to alarm you," he began.

Now in my experience, anyone who starts a sentence with "Now I do not mean to alarm you," is about to say something unpleasant. In fact, he did not need to alarm me, on account of the fact that I was already dangling in a cage above a stinking pit. There was nothing to do but wait for the bad news.

"Once it gets your scent, it will not give up," he said. This was exactly the sort of thing I was worried about. So it would follow me around like a foul smell. In fact, that is not a good way to put it, as it did have a foul smell.

"What in Paws' name is it?" I sighed.

"It is the Boar Horse," came the reply.

"Ah," I replied, "that nasty looking beast that The Micini put on their coins?"

"That's the one," said Curl.

"Anything else you want to tell me?" I asked, already wishing I hadn't.

"Its bite means certain death."

Now there were many questions that I wanted to ask, but so far I had not had a lot of luck with the answers. Before I could get another word out, Curl vanished into the night.

"I will return, if I am not slain."

"Many thanks!" I called.

"Hopefully..." he added.

CATILIS XXII

July 22nd

Perhaps the beast was having a night off - for there were no sounds from the pit. But I dared not sleep, afraid that the dreadful thing would attack me at any moment. To pass the hours I turned my best ear towards the hall, where I could hear the Lords of the Micini talking. I learned that the Arch Mewid has been sent for. He will sit at a great chair at the head of their great table. For there will be a great council. Everything is *great* in this land of the Kitons. I am surprised that they do not call it *Great Kitain* and have done with it. Anyway, I was not pleased to learn this news for I have no great love of The Mewids, who are the priests of this land. Now you will find good and bad wherever you look. But there is something about a religion where you must get dressed up in white robes and dance around the woods waving a silver knife that attracts the wrong sort. There was no sign of Curl today. I have said a little prayer to Backus, the God of long odds, that he has not forgotten about me.

CATILIS XXIII

July 23rd

A bad night again. I woke up to the stink of the beast in the air and the sound of it snorting and stamping. I was in terror. Then I remembered the apple that Curl had given me and cast it into the pit. I was dreading this night but thank Peus and any other Gods you like, Curl came back with another apple. I asked him why he was not in the Great hall with the other Lords of the Micini, welcoming the important visitor. He looked at me and sighed. Then he pulled at a wooden torc around his neck. Now every Kiton warrior loves his jewels and will not get out of bed without his torc. These beautiful necklaces are made of the very finest silver, mostly. Sometimes it is said that the torc-maker will throw in some cheap metals from anything that they find lying around - like a broken knife or whatever. The Kitons have a saying about this: "Cheap torc costs knives," or something similar. Anyway, in all my long years in this strange land, I have never seen one made of wood before. Curl always had a sadness about him, more than you'd expect from the foul weather or the general sadness of living in this land.

"Look," said Curl, showing me his wooden torc. "I am landless. Without land you are nothing. That is why I cannot sit at the great table with the others."

"Oh dear," I replied. "How did that happen?"

"I borrowed money on my family's land, and could not pay it back. So I started to gamble, at dice."

"My mother had a saying about gambling," I began.

"I know. Don't throw good money after bad,"

sighed Curl, shaking his head sadly.

"No, in fact it was 'If at first spin, you don't win, bet, bet again!'" I said. In fact my mother had many sayings. 'Don't cross your bridges before you come to them,' was a favourite of hers. She must have said this so many times that it may have angered the Travel Gods, for she was twice swept down the river Tiber in a flash flood.

"What did you need to borrow money for?" I asked.

"Lots of things," sighed Curl. "My wife wanted a villa, in the Roman style, with mosaics, glass and everything. Then she started to collect brushes. You know, the nice ones with the silver handles that all the Roman females are using."

On hearing this, I let out a sigh. Some of the older Kitons I had met were not used to money and would rather swap things than use coins to pay for them.

"So you gave away your family lands in return for glass and cheap brushes?" I said in disbelief.

"Cheap? Did you see the prices they were charging for those brushes?" Curl said sadly. I hung my head at this news. For I am in the brush business, and could have got him a good deal. But before I could reply he pressed his paw to his mouth.

"Silence!" he whispered, pressing an apple into my paw. "I cannot stay. The beast may hear us!"

CATILIS XXIV

July 24th

I woke to the heavy thud, thud, thud, of a great drum. I wonder who would choose to learn the drums when there are musical instruments out there? At any rate, it was a number of Micini warriors.

"Come!" ordered the first drummer. I guessed that they did not plan to throw me into the pit just then. And so it was that I was led up to the great table, where a figure in white robes was sitting on some kind of throne made of wicker. Why the Kitons like to make seats that look like baskets, I will never know. Looking down, I saw that the floor of the hall had been flooded. The warriors sat on tables, carefully keeping their paws dry.

"Behold! The Mirror of Dreams," said the Arch Mewid, for it was he. The drumming and chanting stopped and even the air was still. In the firelight, the shadows played upon the surface of the water and a vision unfolded. I blinked and blinked again, but in the mirror I could see a great throne, and Queen Boudicat on it, asleep. There were Roman soldiers all around her. Auxiliaries by the look of them. One put a cloth over her jaws so she could not cry out. And all the time, her warriors were snoring. The Romans bundled her into a sack and dragged her out through the hole in the wall.

"Kidnappers! The Queen is taken!" cried a great warrior.

"Death to the Romans! Take off the fat heads of the snail eaters!" hissed another. Swords and some of those nasty curvy silver sickles were waved around, cutting the air. The next thing I knew I could feel claws at my throat, so I wiggled and struggled, biting the paw that held me till it let go.

"Die Queen taker!" spat my opponent. I had to duck as a broadsword carved the air above my head. Twisting away from this attack I made a leap for a table, but my jumping is not what it once was, and I fell down with a splash, into the middle of the smoky water. An awful silence filled the hall. I was sure that I had committed some terrible offence by touching the sacred water (which would be typical for the savage religion of this land). An apology to the Arch Mewid was my only chance.

"I am sorry Arch Mewid," I began, "but that big one with the blue face was chasing me!"

"Silence!" hissed the figure in white. "Look! The vision is changing."

Now I could not actually see the vision that he was talking about. For I was standing in the middle of it with my head sticking out of a vase, I am told. But Curl, who saw everything, says that as soon as I touched the water, it began to smoke and the picture changed. Beside a river the colour of slate, stood the smoking remains of a town. No living thing moved, save for a few crows and the odd fat rat. The wind danced alone, in the ruins. As the Arch Mewid helped me up out of the pool, the warriors backed off and looked at me in fear. All except Mane, who's look could have skinned me. He padded forward ready to pounce. So I leapt back, almost to the edge of the pit, where the creature was waiting below in the dark. I could smell it. It was easy to smell.

"Do not touch him! He is to go free," ordered the Arch Mewid.

"Thank you!" I said, almost crying with the relief. Trying to look casual, I padded away from the edge of the pit. "And I suggest you put that THING down there, whatever it is, on a chain, so that it cannot escape."

"We did," said a voice. "It ate it!"

CATILIS XXV

July 25th

The Queen is Red

So the Micini held another *Great Meeting* in the *Great Hall* to decide how to rescue their *Great Queen*. I shall leave out any further *greats* in order to save paper, which is becoming expensive since the wasp trouble over in Fleagypt, where it is made.

The sun went round the sky in her chariot, as the arguments raged. Her sister, the Moon, was just coming out and they were still talking. Mane shouted they should get up an army and go out and rescue the Queen. This was agreed, but first they needed to decide on a leader. Many wanted to be leader and their shouts were loud enough to wake the gods on Mount Olympus - or wherever the gods of the Micini live. Let us hope for the gods' sake that it is somewhere with thick walls, for the racket was terrible. Then, after hours of this din, someone asks a question.

"Who will pay the wages of the warriors? This question was a killer, for wars cost a lot of money. The biscuit bill alone can be enormous. After more talk, the Arch Mewid said that it was right that the leader of the tribe should pay the warriors' wages. So then each cat who had wanted to be the leader fell silent. Now nobody wanted to be in charge. Unnoticed, a shabby looking form padded into the room.

This unlucky creature had been splashed about the face with red paint, in mockery of the Micini's blue war paint. At first I thought it was a starved rat, for it was thin as a bone - with its ribs sticking out. On seeing this sight, Curl, who was sitting next to me, gave out a shriek.

"Queen Boudicat!" he cried in horror. For it was the Queen, now wearing rags, with her silver torc stolen. She had been shaved from nose to tail. At first the warriors were too shocked to speak. At last a voice spoke out:

"Who has done this to our Queen? Name them, so we can curse them when we take their heads off and send them to Winterspit." There was a great cheer at this.

"Curl," I asked. "What is Winterspit?"

"The opposite of Summerlands," he replied.

"I see," I said, forgetting that *Summerlands* is the Kiton's name for place that you go to when you die.

"Is it nice in Winterspit?" I asked.

"No!" hissed Curl, giving me a dark look. "In Rome, you would call it hell." Now the Queen spoke up.

"My warriors. I hope you have been busy while I've been gone." The Lords of the Micini did not answer.

"Is our army strong and ready for war? I trust that we are ready. But my ears must be deaf. For I cannot hear sword or claw being sharpened."

There followed a guilty silence. No one dared to

open their mouth as the Queen paced up and down the hall like a tiger at the Circus. Stopping next to Mane, she asked:

"Are my eyes blind? For I see no war chariots parked outside my hall?"

At last, the Arch Mewid spoke up:

"They are not yet ready for war with Rome, Queen Boudicat."

"Not ready?" said the Queen, in mock surprise. "Why not? I would throw myself and my daughters into that pit, rather than live under Roman boot!"

"Your warriors could not decide who would be the leader. And many here are worried about the cost of a war," said the Arch Mewid.

When she heard this, Boudicat sprang to the far side of the hall, right up to the very edge of the pit. There was a gasp, as some feared she would throw herself in. Instead she smiled and called out in a soft voice:

"Good females of the Micini tribe, come here to me, your sister." From out of the crowd, came many females, who had been waiting patiently all day whilst the males were arguing. Now they padded over to Boudicat's side of the hall. Amongst them I saw a sad sight. The Queen's own daughters had also been shaved.

"Sisters," said the Queen, "who shall lead our army into battle?"

"You of course, Queen Boudicat," answered a

young tabby, no older than the Queen's youngest daughter. Boudicat smiled, and turning to the males, she roared:

"DID YOU HEAR THAT, WARRIORS?"

Looking up, I saw those warriors trembling. Whether it was with fear or shame, I cannot say. Then suddenly she was calm again. Boudicat walked on until she came to the oldest female in the group. A fat old ginger.

"Listen!" commanded the Queen. And the whole hall fell silent.

"Sister, tell me, who shall pay for this war?"

"The Romans will pay for it," hissed the old one, "With their blood!"

So the warriors of the Micini were shamed by the females of their tribe. I am sure that it was not the first time. They are known to be strong willed and lovers of a good fight, and not just watching one either. I should know, for I married one. It is also true that a rumour got about the camp that the Romans were going to call in their loans, and ask for their money back. Many of the Micini had borrowed money from a Roman called Senicat, and the thought of having to pay it all back put the fear of their Gods into them. As it would mean losing their lands. For these reasons there were no more arguments about what to do next. Queen Boudicat was going to war. It was to be a single blue female and her warriors against the might of The Feline Empire.

CATILIS XXVI

July 26th

Out of the Blue

I am not overjoyed to be marching with this furious queen. Still, at least I am not marching against her. As the army took to the road, I was happy to see a friendly face in the crowd.

"Spartapud!" called Curl, for he had got it into his head that this was my name, and now it had stuck and he would not be told otherwise. We talked as we marched, and I asked him a question that had been bothering me since that dark night when I was caged in the pit.

"What were the Micini doing borrowing money from the Romans? What did they need to buy? In Peus name don't say it was brushes again!"

"All sorts of things," he replied. "Glass for our bowls, jewels, comfortable cushions and mints to make our coins. The Romans were very pleased to lend us the money, at first."

"I bet they were," I replied. "So you are not the only one to have traded lands for silly bits and pieces." Curl nodded sadly.

"We didn't know that they'd want to be paid back twice the amount."

"In my land, a poet called Ferres said that you need three fortunes in this life. One to make your way, another for bribes and the last for your old age." Curl looked at me and fell about laughing

"What is so funny?"

"You and I have saved a fortune," he cried.

"For at least we will not have to worry about growing old."

AUGUSTPUSS I

August 1st

Revolting Shopkeepers.

Today was a day of drizzle. Typical Kittish marching weather. It has been hard going. What is a march but a trudge with the added element of danger? Boudicat's army was winding its way onwards, getting bigger and bigger as it went on through the villages. As we marched, the females and their young sang a song that went like this.

> *"Crackle and spit,*
> *crackle and spit,*
> *orange and pink and red*
> *Crackle and spit,*
> *crackle and spit,*
> *jump right out of your bed."*

"That is a merry tune," I said. And indeed it was the catchiest thing I had ever heard in this tuneless land.

"I will teach it to you," said Curl. And soon I was joining in with the rest of them, singing as I marched.

"What do the words mean?" I asked.

"It is about burning down the houses of our enemies," said Curl. "When a house is put to the torch, the colours of the fire are orange and pink and red.

"I like the jumping bit, where the Romans are burned from their beds and it makes them jump," added a young warrior. On second thoughts, I will leave the singing to the others.

CLAWDIUS THE ODD

I have been called to a meeting with Queen Boudicat. She has an enormous blue tent with many poles and bits of rope everywhere. It is a good job she has slaves, for it must be devil to put up and take down every day. Inside, the Queen was in a good mood, as she had spent the morning shouting at her warriors.

"I have been thinking," she began. "I must know my enemy. Tell me about your young Emperor. Is he a warrior?"

"Not really, great Queen," I began, "he is said to spend all of his time making music and poems."

"That is foolish, especially for a god."

"He is not a god, great Queen. Perhaps you are thinking of the old Emperor, Clawdius?"

"Yes, Clawdius was a god, was he not?" asked Boudicat, with a glare. Now before answering that question, my heart sank. For it would be death if my true views on this ever get out. Officially Clawdius has risen to Mount Olympuss to take his place with Mewpiter and all the others. So I was careful with my answer.

"They are building a mighty temple in his name, with an enormous statue," I replied. The Queen's eyes flashed.

"Where is this temple of the Roman God?"

"In the city of Camulod, great Queen. In fact, my house is just around the corner."

There was a long silence, and the Queen's tail began to flick.

"Do you plan to visit the statue, when it is finished?"

"No," said the Queen. "I plan to ride my chariot over the Roman God's head until all that unhappy town is turned to dust. Then I will scatter the dust in a pile, so that my chariot dogs can use it as their toilet. That is what I plan to do."

"I see!" I replied, with a nervous laugh. Mane, who had been standing nearby, grabbed me by the throat and held me in the air.

"Why do you laugh Roman?" he hissed. I thought that he would kill me on the spot, but a look from the Queen stopped him in his tracks.

That night I learned that Mane got a roasting from the Queen for attacking me. I was honoured to receive a gift - from Boudicat herself. They say that she finds me, "Quite amusing." This is most unusual, I am told. She has even left a small pot in my tent. I was excited to open it, but then I found out that it contains a very foul smelling blue cheese. The food in Boudicat's army is worse than the food in the legions

AUGUSTPUSS V

August 5th

Camulod Crash

Today before dawn we drew near to the city of Camulod, My heart sank as the sun rose. I could think of nothing but our beautiful villa - which stands between Boudicat and her target. Our home was crafted in the finest mud. It even has a mud mosaic. What will my wife say if she returns from Rome to find it ruined? We have other houses, but that will not calm her. I can hear her sharpening her claws now.

"That was our biggest and finest house! And you let them trample it to the ground, you spineless old fool."

If our house is gone, it will be of little comfort if I am still here.

AUGUSTPUSS VI

August 6th

I don't know much about how war works in this strange land. So I have decided to ask Curl whether the town will be destroyed completely (and my house with it!) Your average Roman general these days would cut off the town's water and food, then close down the roads and wait for hunger and thirst to win the battle. But these Kiton warriors fight like we Romans did back in the days of the Repurrblic. In those days the two armies would march off to an open plain outside the city walls and knock the fur off each other. The slaughter would be terrible, but at least no houses would be destroyed in the battle.

AUGUSTPUSS VII

August 7th

Today we have stopped marching. We can see the walls of Camulod. It is a pity that the walls are only half built - for there was no money left to pay the builders. So they went to work on the statue of Clawdius instead.

Curl and I climbed to a tiny hill, to get a better view. Before me I could see the might of Boudicat's army. And nearby I was surprised to see an even larger army. A huge crowd had come - including the very old and the very young. The young ones sang the burning song again, it is so catchy that I found myself humming it without even thinking. Curl bought a dozen oysters from a passing seller and took a place by my side.

"Nice turn out!" he purred.

"What are they all doing here?" I asked.

"What do you mean?" he laughed, sucking on a big oyster and passing me a roasted dormouse. It could have done with a little more salt but it was not bad.

"Won't this crowd get in the way of your army when the fighting starts?"

"Nope," said Curl, licking his paws.

"They might get themselves hurt when the stones and arrows start flying," I added.

"Don't worry," smiled Curl. "They've brought their hats."

Curl padded off to buy another dozen oysters. These Kitons were turning war into a fun day out for all the family. And by the way they are stuffing their faces, they'll have finished their snacks before the show begins.

"What do Roman families do when there's a cranking great battle about to start?" asked Curl, coming back with his prize.

Now, I did think at this time that most of Rome's battles are fought in other countries.

"I don't really know. I suppose they just stay at home and wait," I answered.

Curl roared with laughter.

"Stay at home? They're not going to be much use to you there are they?"

I must have looked puzzled at this, for he went on: "This lot are our loyal supporters - it's nice for the fighters to see a friendly face, to cheer us on."

"So they're here to cheer you on." I asked.

"Well - and there's the looting."

Now, I have never been very noble-minded. But the habit of stalking around the battlefield going through the pockets of the dead, makes me feel quite sick. Not that it does not go on in the Roman legions too. But to encourage your family to join in! It was all that I could do to stop myself spitting in disgust.

"And they like doing this grim work, your females, your old and your young ones?" I asked.

"They look forward to the looting," said Curl. "If the gods are willing, a fight day is a great day out with free shopping afterwards."

"I see," I replied.

The gods must have given me a face that is easy to read, for I have always found it hard not to show my feelings.

"Or there's *The Whisperers*," said Curl. "If looting is not your thing, you can join *The Whisperers*."

AUGUSTPUSS VIII
August 8th

Careless Whisperer

Now, maybe Fortune has spun me a good one. For this morning I asked the Queen about *The Whisperers* and she has said I am to join them.

"You will learn that the tongue can be as sharp as the sword," she said.

"Whatever you have in mind great Queen, I hope it does not involve a lot of licking. For I burnt my tongue on a dormouse kebab last night," I answered.

AUGUSTPUSS XIII
August 13th

Here I sit, surrounded by ruins. As there is little else to do, I shall now bring my diary up to date. Well, I did not much like the sound of joining any group, but it is not a good idea to say 'No' to a Queen. Especially not to a warrior Queen. On hearing that I was to join *The Whisperers*, one warrior, who was practising his battle-cry, began to laugh so much that he almost cut himself on his broadsword.

So as the Queen's army made ready for war, we *Whisperers* were told to meet in a little patch of flowers near the gap at the far end of the city wall. I arrived to find the place empty, except for a large female who was busy packing fish into a basket. Not knowing if she was one of our group, I crept up to her and in my quietest voice I whispered.

"Is this the right place?"

"What?" replied the large one, slapping her last carp into the basket. In a hushed voice I said again:

"Is this the right place? For... *The Whisperers?*"

"Weirdling!" she hissed. And without another word of warning, she beat me around the face with a sizable trout. She followed this up with a slap from a large carp that she got from her basket. With no more fish available, she pounced and knocked me to the ground. When I came to my senses, she was sitting on top of me. Getting up was out of the question, for this cat had a rear end the size of Londump and its surrounding villages.

"What do you want strange one? Speak up before I give you another thrashing."

"The Whisperers," I puffed, in as normal a voice as I could manage, "the Queen has sent me to join them." There was a laugh from the crowd that had gathered to watch.

"All right," said the fat one, letting me go. "But you'd better speak plainly instead of mumbling like that. There are some quick tempers amongst us Micini."

It was then that I noticed that the crowd around me was entirely made up of females.

"Sorry. I thought that we had to speak in a whisper in this group."

"Silly!" laughed the large one, whose name was Spitlia. "How would the enemy hear what we want them to hear if we went around mumbling all the time?" And soon we were given our orders. We were to go into the town and spread lies about the strength of Queen Boudicat and the terrible pawtents against the Romans. For soldiers of any land are very super-stitious, believing in ghosts and signs and the like. In short, they are very easily spooked. Even our lads of the legions. So we whispered to the Romans that Boudicat was a witch, who ate white snakes for breakfast, lunch and dinner. We swore that all who fought against her would be cursed. We told them that the Queen's army was six hundred thousand strong and had already taken Londump. Strange howling noises had been heard in the theatre. And that Governor Mewtonius was mad, and had a wooden leg and a lazy eye. And finally, we said that an old soldier had seen a vision - of the statue of the Goddess Victory falling down, as if she was running away. That idea was mine and I think the others liked it very much. In fact, I found myself very good at the whispering game. And in this way our stories spread about the town from shop to shop and from house to house. And the tails of the Romans hiding in that city went down, but Boudicat's supporters grew bolder. As the day grew darker, we were all told to go off and do a last bit of whispering, as the time for the battle drew near.

"Say whatever you like as long as it's nasty," said Spitlia. "And if you can't think of anything bad to say, don't say anything at all!"

Now I have lived in the town of Camulod for many years and I should know the streets well. But I have never been very good at directions, or remembering the names of streets. Who needs a map when you have servants, I always say. Nevertheless, I had a plan of my own. I would find my way back to my dear mud mansion and bury my valuables before the fighting started. I was padding carefully down Troutling Street, when I saw an old female dashing towards me.

"Run for your life!" she cried. "Boudicat is upon us. Run before her beast eats you alive!"

Now, on hearing this I laughed out loud. For this was a very good one indeed. I felt slightly annoyed not to have thought of it myself. It was now totally dark. The sky above the town was black as the townsfolk had buried all their valuables - including their lamps and oil. I made for the main road leading up towards the temple. As I turned the corner, I smelt it. A funny smell, somewhat piggish! My blood froze, for I had smelled something like it back at the Queen's Hall. Then I heard a snort in the darkness ahead of me.

"Hello?" I called. I frantically searched my pockets for apples.

"SSNNNNNNNORRRT!" came a sound. Out from behind a water-trough stepped the beast. It was a gingery red colour, with bristles running in a ridge along its back and great tusks, somewhat yellow around the root.

"Thank Peus for that!" I cried. For it was not the beastly Boar Horse that had haunted my dreams as I dangled over that foul pit. It was a wild boar, plain and simple.

Now it is said that when you are face to face with a wild animal, it is best to show it who is the boss. Stand tall. Be still. Avoid sudden movements. Speak out in a strong voice. Never let it see that you are afraid. Play the master.

I turned tail and ran. I can say that I have not run like that in many years. I was faster than Purrcury, the messenger of the Gods, on a same-day delivery. I wandered where the streets have no names - or the kind of names that it would not be respectable to write down in this diary. I am not the runner that I was in my youth, but fear of being tusked to death is a great trainer and would have the laziest of us out of their basket. At last, I slowed down to a trot. Padding around a corner, I found my self face-to-face with a terrible scene. By running here and there, I had arrived back at Matling street - at the far end by the temple path. Looking down this long straight street I saw a sight to make Roman blood run cold. I was face to face with a blue mob, screaming murder and death to the Emperor, the Governor and any other Romans they could think of. They prowled down the streets putting shops and, more worryingly, houses to the torch as they went. As their cries hit my ears, bitter smoke from the fires brought tears to my eyes. So I turned tail and ran up the path towards the temple, with the mob not far behind. At last, I reached the top of the track and came out in front of the temple. The great statue of Clawdius towered above me, wrapped in ropes and ladders. I almost tripped over a sign saying:

UNDER CONSTRUCTION.

"Halt, in the name of Rome!" came a shout. An old legionary jumped into my path, claws out, sword at the ready, spoiling for a fight.

"Stop friend!" I cried. "I am a freed-cat, a Roman myself." The old soldier eyed me carefully. My Catin was still good, but my clothes were spattered with mud, and an odd mixture of Roman and Kittish styles. He gave me a sideways look and slowly licked a gnarled paw. An old war wound perhaps. The sound of shouting broke the silence.

"Hurry! I have forty thousand Kitons and a savage beast at my tail."

"Mewpiter save us! That many?" said the Scenturian slowly. "Follow me if you must, or find your own hiding place."

In a couple of leaps he disappeared up the poles and ropes that surrounded the chest and paws of Clawdius's statue. I said a silent prayer to Agrippa - the god of long drops - that I would not fall. He was attacking the climb at such a pace, it was all that I could do to keep up with him. Leap followed leap and we were soon at a little trap door at the base of my old master's ear. I noticed that they had left out a little bald patch, which he always used to lick. I struggled to open the trap door. Clawdius always did have a wax problem. At last we heaved our way in and I found myself in a dark chamber. I could hear my steps echo out above me.

"What news of the enemy?" asked a voice from the

darkness.

"The savages are on their way," said the Scenturian.

"Shall we pull the ladders up?" asked the voice.

"Save your strength and say your prayers. There are forty thousand of them."

"Great Paws have mercy!" came a cry. "That many?" "What news of the Hisspania?"

Apparently, the Romans had heard a rumour that the Legion of the IX Hisspania Auxiliaries were said to be on their way from Londump, led by General Feralis. I said I had no news of that mad lot - who are said to be the wildest troops in this savage land. On hearing that no help was on the way, the mood of the room, already low, sank to the depths.

"Will you defend the walls?" I asked. A grim laughter echoed around the room.

"The walls are not finished. The good citizens of Camulod would not pay their taxes. There's only fifty of us old soldiers here," hissed the Scenturian. "We couldn't defend a fish market. The town is as good as lost."

"We can only wait for the end," said a voice from the dark, even more miserable than the others.

"That doesn't sound very bright," I said.

"I told you not to follow me," came the reply. Suddenly, an idea popped into my mind. These soldiers were few in number. But they were hardened by years of battles in the legions. They were old, but they were a band of brothers. A band of miserable, squabbling brothers - but brothers still. If only someone could inspire them with a good speech! Perhaps with Fortune's help, he could help them win an incredible victory. The right leader could turn death to glory. My eyes, now used to the dark, met theirs. All looked at me, waiting for my next word.

"Where is the way out?" I asked. For I have never been much of a leader. I slipped out of a plate in the neck of the statue of the God Clawdius and peeped down on the burning town. I saw a sight that will haunt my dreams forever. Luckily, I cannot remember my dreams, so if any haunting is going on, it does not worry me. What I saw, was a screaming mob, tearing up the city brick by brick and shaking the thick walls of the temple with their rage. In the centre of the storm, hissing like a demon, was the Micini's terrible Queen. If I can only get to Boudicat, I thought, I could have some protection from the mob. But it would be death to take one pace into the crowd. It would also mean death to get caught here with the Roman defenders. So I found myself trapped. But not for long. There was a whistling hiss and a crash, and the wooden scaffold below me lit up light a bonfire. Taking a big breath, I offered myself to the Goddess Fortune. I had a feeling that she wouldn't want me. And so it proved, as I made the long jump across to Clawdius' right paw. Sadly, many eyes were looking at the statue of Rome's newest God that day.

"There! Get the fat one. Death to the snail-eater!" came a shout. Now I am not as slim as I was in my youth, but it did not take me long to realise that I'd been spotted. I span around and came face to face with a party of Kiton warriors. They were blue from head to tip of tail but they had a white heron symbol on their long shields. They were not Micini, but a hunting party from some other tribe, out to join the fun. They eyed me as a snake looks at a baby bird in the nest. It would not be long now. They only had to knock me from my perch. Now my friend Russell back at the Spa in Rome said that it was always best to look for the good in everything. "There's a tasty meal inside every clam," he used to say. But as I wobbled on my narrow ledge, I was finding it hard to see the good in this fix. It is a good job they are not archers, I thought. A small shower of arrows would send me crashing down. The leader of the Kitons gave a shout and all at once the rest began to scrabble and scratch about on the ground. "Are they looking for mice?" I wondered, daring to hope that they might go off and leave me alone. When they got up, each warrior clutched a rock in his paw. They threw these at me in great showers, so that I could not hide. I took a hit on the front paw and another below the collar. The force of these stinging blows left me clinging by a single claw. I tried to swing to safety, but it was useless. The next well-aimed stone would send me crashing to my death. Time slowed to a waddle. I thought of my son.

There is so much he needs to know about this world. It was a shame that I have taught him almost nothing of any practical use. I wished that he could throw a rock like that. My thoughts turned to my dear wife. At least I would not have to explain to her that her favourite house had been crushed and burned to a crisp by a Kiton uprising.

FLY AWAY HOME

Just then, I heard the sound of beating wings above my head. I looked up and saw a great white bird. I wondered for a moment if it was the Heron King, about to fly me to Summerlands. For the Kitons think this bird is a god. With this thought, I let go of my hold and fell. Now it is said by the Micini that a Roman will always land on his paws. And it is true that Fortune gave me two amazing spins at this time. For the Kitons had gathered up a lot of straw and brushwood and piled it around the town walls ready to put them to the torch. Boudicat must have ordered the same for the statue of Clawdius, because I landed head first in a pile of sticks. You may ask why I did not simply jump down onto this pile earlier. But from where I was sitting on the ledge, I could not get a clear view of it. This was Fortune's first lucky spin. I found myself still on my paws - with no broken bones - at the base of the statue. At the time I was not pleased, for I knew that the Herons were about to pounce. Was it better to die skewered on a spear or fall from a great height? But when I looked down in their direction, I gave thanks to every God on Mount Olympuss and a few others besides, even old Clawdius himself. For as soon as the warriors caught site of the heron, they followed it. For it was the law of their tribe to follow the Heron King. In fact, it was not the Heron King, but a bird that had taken an interest in the fish pool behind the statue of Clawdius. At any rate, they had taken off after the heron, and now I was alone, still as death, in a pile of sticks. I pulled some more straw over me in order to hide myself from the Kitons. For as I have said - their supporters were going about the town and stealing anything they could get their claws on from the bodies of the fallen. And if a Roman was not dead, but just injured, then these 'supporters' would finish him off with a club or a big stick, before taking his money. So it seemed a very good idea to be out of sight. As I lay hidden in my little nest of sticks, I decided to rest for a minute. I was still in terrible fear of my life. It is said that fear plays funny tricks on us. Fear of death makes me terribly hungry. I reached into a pocket and I found it empty. I tried another - with the same result. In my last pocket I came across the little jar of blue cheese that Boudicat had given me. I got the lid off in an instant and had a lick. It tasted bitter, worse than I remembered.

At that point, I heard a voice in my head. Now, all of us hear voices in our heads, which are nothing much to worry about. My voice says things like, "That cushion looks comfy." Or "Fish for dinner would be nice." In this way I hold a little conversation with myself about the details of the day. Whenever my little voice speaks, I can hear it as clear as a xylophone. Now - it is important to listen to this little voice. But it is also important to learn to ignore it if it says things like "You are too fat," or "You will never do anything well." Mine is often saying this sort of thing. So it was not a surprise to hear a voice in my head saying:

"Stop!"

I knew in an instant, that the voice inside my head was not my own. I took another lick at the blue cheese.

"Stop licking that." It wanted me to stop licking the cheese. "That is not cheese!" it said, becoming angry.

"Wode." It went on wearily, answering my next question ("What is it then?") before I had asked it.

"Hurry, for there is little time," it said.

"Tefnut!" I cried in amazement, for I knew the voice of my old friend. Well - perhaps not really a friend, more of a teacher and mystic. "Where have you been all these years? And why are you in my head?" I asked.

"I would rather not answer that," she hissed. "Now rub the blue cream all over your body. Unless you care to join me in this place."

"Rub cheese into my coat," I whined. "Whatever for? Will the smell of it keep the enemy at bay?"

Tefnut did not answer. "Is it magic cheese then?" I

asked. "Why have you gone all quiet?"

"On this side, we feel nothing. Love, hate, joy and pain are out of our reach, far behind the grave. We watch, but we feel nothing."

"Oh dear," was all that I could think of to say.

"So how come you are ANNOYING ME even now?" she hissed. "Put the wode on now."

Of course, Tefnut was right. It was not cheese - but wode - the blue battle paint of the Kiton warriors. For the Queen to give it to me as a present, was a great gift. And I had been carrying it around in my pocket all along. It is a good job that I did not find a biscuit on my travels. I'd just finished rubbing it on when a crackling noise made my whiskers twitch. Then I heard Tefnut's voice for the last time. I call her in my dreams sometimes but she never answers. I remember the last word that she ever spoke to me.

"Run!" she said.

TORCHED WOOD

The Queen's army were busy putting the statue of Clawdius to the torch. Now I was caught like a field mouse in the burning stubble. Scrambling at the twigs, I heaved myself up and out of the trench. Coughing in the sunlight, I was now face-to-face with a huge Micini warrior holding a rake.

"Fool!" he hissed. "This is no time for ratting. Didn't your mother warn you not to play with fire?"

In fact my mother loved burning things and would

often leave me to amuse myself, rubbing at sticks to see if they would burn. But I thought that this would be a bad time to bring up my family history. So I made my excuses and sloped off down the temple path.

"Oi!" came a shout that stopped me dead in my tracks. In a panic I wondered if I had put enough wode on my back. Slowly, I turned to face my accuser.

"Yes?" I asked, trying to sound care free.

"The Queen is down the North track. You don't want to get lost," called a burly warrior, with a face like a cracked vase.

"Thanks!" I replied, promising to do the Goddess Fortune a proper sacrifice next time.

"Get moving brother! The Queen'll have your ears for piggy slippers if you come back late."

So I set off down the temple path as he'd suggested, although I already knew exactly where I was going. I had remembered my beautiful mansion, and my plan. I must get back there, dig a big hole and bury anything of value in the courtyard. That would stop the looters getting their thieving claws on my things.

BROKEN HOME

I arrived to a sorry sight. My fine mansion was now a crushed molehill. All my treasures had been stolen, including my fish collection and my collection of rare brushes. The sky God Mewpiter had not been kind. A thunderstorm rained troubled water all over the things the looters didn't take. My mud mosaic was ruined too. Perhaps I should have put a picture of the god Mewpiter on it instead of the god Purcurry.

As I sat in my puddle, I was surprised to hear Curl's voice.

"Cheer up!" he said. Now, there are many things you could say to an old cat who has seen his life's work burnt and then washed into a muddy puddle. But "Cheer up!" perhaps is not the best.

"Neptuna's weeds!" I cried. "It is all ruined!" Curl smiled. "Never mind, you won't need houses where we're going!"

I forced a smile. Curl was a sight. I don't know what he'd trodden in, but the blue wode on his paws had turned to the yellow colour of the vomitorium. I forgot my worries for a moment and laughed. Then I made a little pile of the few things that I could save from the wreck of my house.

For one good thing, my dining table still stood and on it my little shrine to Fortune, who used to be my favourite goddess. I looked at her statue, which showed her sitting at her spinning wheel and I wondered what she had in store for me. I have had some ill luck since my wife left for Rome. But at least this was not our only home. For we have a loft in Londump and a mansionette in Matling St, where we stay when visiting my wife's family in the wild north. We have had extra reeds put on the roof as the weather gods are not often happy up there. The sky is always crying. Sometimes if you are lucky, the sky god spits down hail stones the sizes of dove eggs. It is nice to have a change from the rain sometimes.

LANDLESS LORD

As Curl is always talking about being 'landless,' I thought it best not to tell him about my other houses. I looked at his puffy face for a minute and smiled. Then I had a thought.

"Tell the Queen that I have a message for her," I said, leaping up.

"You can tell her yourself, look!" laughed Curl, pointing through what used to be my kitchen to a line of flags coming up the road. A mighty war chariot, pulled by two white dogs, came hoving into sight, its huge wheels grinding into the rubble of my house. Its speed was amazing. For a moment I thought that it would not stop but, at the last minute the driver hauled on the reins and brought the left dog round in a spinning turn. With a crash, the chariot smashed into my table and my little statue of Fortune was broken under the wheels. Seeing what she'd done, the Queen pulled to a halt, sprang down and carefully picked up the pieces of the broken god.

"I am sorry about your hovel, Sister's daughter's husband," said Boudicat. At this, I almost bristled. I nearly pointed out that it was once the best mud mansion in all of Camulod, made entirely of local materials. But before I could get the words out, the Queen continued.

"Do not fear, for I will have my carpenters build you another hovel when we have won."

Carefully, she placed the Goddess Fortune's broken wheel into my paw.

"Great Queen," I began. For I now had something difficult to say. "Wouldn't it be best to see sense! Flee over the sea to Maul or something? You have won a victory today, but you cannot mean to take on Rome?"

"Can't I?" she laughed. And all her host began to shake with laughter too. "Is this all you have to tell me, Sister's daughter's husband?" She caught my gaze, her thick tail flicking and her amber eyes shining like lamps. I lowered my voice to a whisper - for what I had to say was for her ears alone. Despite myself, I found myself betraying Rome, the city I had grown up in. There was something magnificent about this Queen. No wonder a hundred thousand had left their crops to rot in the field in order to join her adventure.

"While I was in the temple I overheard some soldiers talking. The news is bad. The Ninth Hisspania are coming. They are too late to save the city, but that will not bother them. They are Rome's wildest troops. We send the Auxiliaries in first, when we don't want to risk spilling Roman blood. And they are coming now, on the East road."

Boudicat looked at me proudly. She sensed how serious the thing that I was doing.

"The East road. That is where you have sent the

old and the females is it not?" I asked. Boudicat smiled and raised her spear aloft.

"The females are with me!" she cried. Her followers cheered, some of them trampling the rest of my walls for good measure. By their voices I heard that a good deal of the Micini females had come to war with the males. Boudicat gave a purr of approval and smiled.

"You have done well, sister's daughter's husband! But fear not, for the Roman beasts are CONQUERED ALREADY!" These last words were given in a cry that shook the rest of my walls to dust. I looked on, hardly believing my eyes, as she slammed a pole into the ground in front of me. On top of this pole was an Eagle, it was the standard of the Ninth Hisspania.

I gasped, for I knew that no legion gives up its Eagle without a bitter fight. To return to Rome without your Eagle is to come back lower than a slave even. Boudicat caught the horror in my gaze and laughed louder.

"Now, are you going to sit there, as useful as a bone in a fishcake - or are you coming to WAR! WITH ME!!!"

On hearing this the Micini warriors around her gave out another mighty cheer and started dancing in the street, trampling my things into the mud as they danced.

"Wait! That cost me a fortune," I moaned, trying to rescue a sports collar that I had bought for my son at great expense. But I was powerless to stop their pounding blue paws. You cannot deny that they would follow Boudicat to the end of the Earth. In their case, it is a journey so short that they will not need their packed lunches.

AUGUSTPUSS XX

August 20th

The Lady is for Burning

As I write, I am camping out under the stars on Matling St, or 'Main Road' as the Kitons call it. I am headed for Londump in a hurry, but I have stopped to avoid the black flies. They bite harder at this time in the afternoon. The Queen and the Micini army are behind me. Hopefully, they are far behind me. Perhaps I should explain. As I have said, it is hard to say 'No' to a Queen, and to a warrior Queen doubly so. But greater than the fear of Queen Boudicat is the fear of my own wife. What will she say when she returns from Rome and finds our beautiful mud mansion all smashed and trampled into the dust? It is likely that she will not say anything but she'll have my hide for her umbrella. The Fleagyptians have a saying - milk cannot taste sweet until you've tasted dust. Well, now I have tasted enough dust - thank you very much. I must take better care of the houses I have left. An idea came to me when I was helping Curl back to his tent.

For he had been on the catnip all night.

"Out of the way Spartapud! I'm off home," he cried, crashing into a pile of shields.

"Are you all right?" I asked. For he did not look very steady on his paws.

"Never better, Spartapud," he answered. But I could smell the catnip on his breath.

"Can you walk in a straight line?" I asked.

"No! But I could do you two circles!"

As we neared his tent, he began to cry.

"Poor landless Curl and homeless Spartapud. Brother – you and me are just the same!"

"Yes. Well, not quite," I answered. "I still have my loft in Londump." At this point, I thought it best not to mention my Matling St Mansionette or my field in Ferulanium.

Now, as we were talking, a group of Micini Lords were coming down the path and overheard me. "Londump! Londump!" cried one of their number, and more cheers came back to answer. Then, I felt a claw on my shoulder.

"Hey, Roman. Do you get a good view of the Tower of Londump from your house?"

This was a strange question, but I decided that it would be rude not to answer.

"Yes," I said proudly." "As long as it is not foggy and the chicken shop next door does not have their fires lit, you can see some of it."

"Not for long," howled the warriors in reply.

Wicked laughter rang out around the camp. Curl did not join in. Perhaps he understands the pain of losing everything you have. Or maybe it was the Catnip, I do not know.

.

THE MUDDY TOWER

The next day, I found out that the Micini will march on the town of Londump. Boudicat has ordered them to trample until the famous Tower is no higher than a mole hill. I am not sure exactly how she plans to measure it.

I was very surprised to find Curl outside my tent in the early dawn, in a frantic state.

"Last night I had a dream," he said.

"Giant hairless mice with two heads on one body again?" I asked. "It is the catnip, I am sure of it. You need to cut down."

"No," he cried excitedly. "I dreamed about you last night. You went to Londump. And you sold your house."

"Is that all?" I sighed. "No giant mice then?"

"Don't you see?" said Curl. "If you sell the house, it will not matter if it is trampled to dust when we attack Londump."

For a cat who lost his family's lands to a money lender, Curl is a genius. I thanked him, but pointed out the big problem with his idea.

"Isn't the Queen marching on Londump now?" I asked.

"Not yet," said Curl. "First we must feast. That'll be a four day job. Then it'll be Wooolsday – we never march on a Wooolsday. And before we can go, we need to meet the other tribes – the Trinos and the Catres. That'll mean more feasting. They're big eaters, those gingers."

Now I was stunned to hear this news. For Governor Mewtonius must be sailing from the Island of Moaner, (or Angle-sea as the locals call it, because of the good fishing). I am no military mastermind but I should say that the Queen's only chance would be to rush to Londump, attack, and run away, as if the hordes of Scruffio were at her tail. I explained all this to Curl, and even tried to make a little drawing in the mud.

"I have thought about what you say," he answered. "But our Mewids made promises to the Great Mother - the Goddess Andrasta the Unconquerable.

"Andrasta might be Unconquerable, but the Mewids aren't, are they?" I replied. "They don't do any of the actual fighting, but you've lost a lot of battles for them, haven't you?" Curl sank to the ground and sulked, so I apologised.

"Still, we cannot leave till they are ready," he said. I did not try to argue. But while the Micini's Mewids are busy waving their silver sickles about, the Romans will get together a large army. That may be the end of Boudicat and the Micini. On the good side, there may be time for me to sell my Londump Loft before the Queen's army gets their torches lit.

AUGUSTPUSS XXII

August 22nd

I arrived at the Gate of Londump to find a long queue in front of me. When we first came to their land, these Kitons knew nothing about queues. Now there are queues all over the land. At least we Romans have given them something. When I arrived at the front of the line, I heard something buzz past my left ear. I jumped back, for the flies in this land have daggers for teeth. Then I felt another buzz. I looked up to see two slingers on the walls - firing stones at me.

"Stop! Stop!" I cried, dancing left and right whilst thanking Paws that they were such poor shots. I pulled out the key to my house and held it up so that they could see it.

"I am a loft house owner. I pay my taxes, let me pass!" But my leaping around attracted more stones. The louder I shouted, the faster they fired. Soon a lively crowd gathered to watch, and some of those rascals joined in with the stoning - shouting:

"Teach the stranger how to dance!"

Now, I do not think that these stone thrower had traditional Kittish dancing in mind when they said this. I leaped about in a panic, trying to dodge their stones but was hit several times before I turned tail and ran. I took shelter behind the town sign. It said:

Londump: we're in it together

LOFT LIVING

It was only after I had washed all of the blue wode out of my coat that I was able to get past the slingers at the gates. In my haste to get into the city, I had forgotten to brush it out. When they let me in, my first port of call was the merchant who had sold me my loft house. His shop was incredibly clean. An old tabby with a bucket was giving the floor a good scrubbing. As I padded up to the desk, the merchant smiled like a snake. When I told him why I'd come, he laughed like a jackal.

"Another one of you with a house for sale? What a pity you didn't come to me sooner. Three months ago, the shop was thick with fools who would pay thirty in gold for a tiny loft house. No bigger than a cupboard!"

"I paid you forty for mine three months ago," I answered, bristling slightly. "What would you give me for it now?" The merchant shook his head and leapt up to the windowsill. He was the sort of shopkeeper who looks on his customers, as you or I might look on a boil we discovered under our collar.

"Come and see," he said. I followed him up. Through the window, I looked out on a long line, made up of both Romans and Kitons, all carrying their things in carts, with chickens and pigeons in baskets. This ragged queue wound on, all the way down to the riverside where the boats were moored.

"If it was a boat that you had to sell, I'd give you a hundred in gold for it," laughed the merchant.

"This is ill news," I said, speaking my thoughts out loud. "It is a disgrace. That's what it is," croaked a cracked voice. The old cleaner looked up from her bucket and let out a hiss.

"They call it the Mighty Feline Empire. And those cringing layabouts won't lift a claw to defend old Londump Town from that Hell Queen and her filthy crew."

"Aren't the Romans going to defend Londump? I thought Governor Mewtonius was on his way," I said.

"Mewtonius," she hissed, spitting out the name like gristle from a mouthful of sausage. "Governor Mewtonius was here already. But he didn't think us worth defending. So he decided to abandon us."

"Mewtonius said that?" I replied, nearly slipping on a wet patch. "He didn't have to say it. Just look for yourself," In the line outside I saw many well-known Romans, waiting for boats. Including The Procurator (whose taxes had caused all this trouble). The old cleaner let out another hiss and got back to her floor, whipping it with a dirty rag. I knew how she felt. It was all right for them. They could sail away into history. We had to eat the dish that they'd prepared for us. I put my key on the table and turned back to the merchant.

"Come now," I begged. "My beautiful loft house. It must be worth something. I would take twenty for it now, if I can have the gold by sundown." But he threw the key back at me. Then he said something about greedy fools who would beg him to take their dog to a fish market and blame him when it does not sell. I had heard enough about markets, so I returned to my worthless loft house to lick my wounds. These were mostly bruises from the stoning. I found the street easily enough and climbed the five flights of stairs - the last three are actually ladders. High above Londump Town, I let out a little purr of relief to be home. I put my key into the lock and gave the door a push but it would not open. Cursing the lock makers of Londump, I gave the door another hard push and clawed at the lock with all my strength but still the key would not turn. How I had being looked forward to a night in a basket, under my own roof. But I was locked out of my own loft. Some time later, I had a thought. I was right. It turned out that the merchant had thrown back the wrong key and given me the key to a fishmongers cellar. Back at the shop, the fishmonger was spoiling for a fight. He was angry with me and the merchant, as he had a large catch of eels getting warm on the streets outside his cellar. But I refused to pay for a single eel. He was most persuasive however. In the end I left with the right key and a bucketful.

As I watched them wiggle in the bucket, I thought of my worthless house. All the effort we had put in to make the earth walls lighter and keep the living area free from personal clutter would be wasted now. How long it would be before Boudicat and her army arrived to put it to the torch. I made a small sacrifice to Fortune and also gave a prayer to Backus, the god of long odds, who also does lost causes.

FORTUNE SPINS ME A GOOD ONE

The next morning I was woken by a knocking that shook my door on its hinges, which had already been damaged from the night before. My prayers had been answered.

Outside the door, stood the merchant. He was quite different from the day before - all smiles and sweetness. He gave me a wink. It seems that there is one customer who has not heard of the war and is looking for a second hut with a view of the Tower of Londump. This buyer was right behind him, coming up the ladder! He even had a bag of gold in his paw. In a panic, the merchant ordered me to go up to my roof garden.

"Whatever for?" I asked.

"To make the room look bigger, you half-wit," he hissed, suddenly his old self again now that he could smell gold. As I climbed the ladder to the roof I heard him in a happy mood again. He could have charmed the scales of Neptuna as he talked about my hardwood floor, solid marble tiles and Roman style underfloor heating. I was curious to see what kind of cat would want to buy a loft in a part of town that was about to become a battlefield? For a moment I felt guilty. It did not seem fair to go through with the sale without telling him. Anyway, I took a peak, but could not see much. The buyer was wearing a long cloak and hood. As they climbed up to the roof, the merchant gave me a second wink. The viewing was going well and the buyer was much taken with my built-in sleeping basket. A sale was 'in the bag'. But then, bad fortune found me out. As the merchant brought up the customer to admire the view, a burning torch landed in my herb garden, singeing my rosemary bush. I was surprised that the merchant ignored the burning bush.

"This is a space fit for the very Gods themselves," he purred. Then he added "And such a beautiful smell of herbs in this well-sized roof garden."

Just then, we heard shouts from the street below and a second flaming torch landed, this time on my lucky holly bush. I wonder what the Mewids would have to say about that, as holly is one of their special plants. The merchant seemed to have finished finding nice things to say about my loft.

"Aaargh! Boudicat is here! Run for your lives," he cried in a panic. On his way down the ladder he tangled with the hooded customer.

"I don't suppose you're interested in making an offer?" he asked. Without waiting for a reply he was down the ladder like a rat down a pipe. By now, the two bushes were starting to crackle as the flames caught hold. Now at this point, I was amazed that the buyer took off his cloak and hood and threw them onto the fire to kill the flames. For a moment, I didn't recognise him - as he was blue from ear to tail.

"Curl!" I cried. "Whatever brings you here?"

"Spartapud, I've found you at last. This is the tenth house I've seen this morning."

"Fortune be praised! I said. "The Micini may be attacking, and my second house will burn. But at least I will be safe with my Micini friend by my side."

"Save your thanks," he said with a frown. "That's not our army out there. It's the Romans."

I ran to edge of my roof screaming, "Romans? Home wreckers! What in Paws name do you think you're doing?"

"I expect they're putting the town to the torch before they leave," said Curl, offering me an oyster. Apparently, you could get a great deal on shellfish at any stall in the city. I padded sadly away from the edge as another burning torch arrived.

"Oh Gods - hear my cries," I sobbed. "My mud mansion is flat as a gnat and if you do not help, my lovely loft will be lost too."

That fickle mistress Fortune seems to have stopped listening to me, so I gave her statue a few biscuits and then moved on to Paws and Mewpiter. But the flames were taking hold. I didn't want to get my coat singed so I called to Curl. We both leapt down the ladder and rolled out coughing in the street.

My lovely loft was burning like an alter. So I thought I'd throw in a few offerings to Kittish gods as well, for good measure - as I needed all the help I could get. My wife had to learn all of them once, for a test - and I remembered many of their strange names. I was ready to go from Abandinit (their river god) to Zacharpuss (who does theft). This last one was worth the trouble. Maybe the land belonged to some Kiton or other before my house was built on it? I was thinking about getting some cheap mistletoe and holly in, when Curl stopped me.

"There is no time for that now," he said. "The Queen has summoned you."

"Can't it wait?" I said, searching my pockets for the oak leaves I'd collected. Curl didn't answer, but gave me a serious look. "I'm sorry," I began.

"My home has been torched. I cannot come running whenever she calls. What in Peus' name does she expect me to do?"

Curl shook his head and gave me a long look.

"She expects you to follow," he said.

"She'd better get her army ready quickly, or it'll be Summerlands for her and all of you with her," I said. Well, in fact this is what I should have said, but I am too old for arguments, and besides, I am fond of Curl. He would have some explaining to do if he returned to Boudicat without me. So I decided to go with him.

AUGUSTPUSS XXX

August 30th

The Curse of Clawdius

Curl and I crept slowly out of that unhappy town, making our way along the river to the north wall. We went as quickly as we dared, not wanting to be caught on the road. As I rounded a turn there was a mighty bang that Mewpiter the Thunderer would have been proud of. I spun around, only to see the Tower of Londump crash into the grey river. The water began to spit and hiss like cheap oil in a lamp.

So Curl and I headed north for the Micini camp. We reached it before three moons had passed. Well, I am guessing that the third moon came and went. For the night was miserable and mist-soaked. It was the sort of night where you should be relaxing in your own basket, not fighting off the ticks in some stone-spangled ditch. The very land itself seemed to be bleeding fog.

Curl was careful not to lead me into these pockets of fog, and not without good reason. Once we followed a line of oaks, wondering if it was a path. He let out a hiss and called to me to turn back, putting himself between me and the first tree. Out of the corner of my eye, I saw a stockade, with trophies and spears, and something else. As the clouds kissed the moon's face, I saw it. First, the symbol of The Boar Horse on a shield. I shivered at the sight of it. The creature seems to haunt my steps. But underneath was something worse, heaped up in little towers of white.

"What is this place?" I whispered.

"We must leave now, this belongs to the Mewids," said Curl. Perhaps Mewlious Caesar was right when he said that the Mewids were as bad as any savages in the Empire. But they had been pushed to extremes these past few years and hunted down by the Governor. Nero himself has passed a law against them and all their ways.

"Come on," hissed Curl. My curiosity will never be the death of me - and I have seen enough bad sights in my times without wanted to add to that list. So I turned and followed Curl into the fog.

The next morning, the fog lifted from the land. Curl and I talked of much on that last day of the journey - but I saved the most important question until our arrival. I knew we'd arrived at the Micini camp because you could smell the catnip kebabs. As we spotted the Queen's tents, I finally asked the question.

"What does Queen Boudicat want with me?" Curl stopped and looked over his shoulder, as if sniffing the air for a scent. I was surprised he could smell anything with the wode pots on the boil again. Curl drew close - close enough for me to see bits of chicken from his breakfast in his teeth.

"The Queen is sick," he whispered. "Some fear that she will die."

"Die?" I cried in amazement.

"SSSSH!" hissed Curl in a rage. "Don't say it out loud, if you value your tongue. If the news gets out we are all finished."

"I doubt that the Romans can hear us," I answered, annoyed that Curl seemed to fly into a temper at the slightest thing. For he was shaking as he glared at me.

"You have lived in this land for many summers." he said seriously. "What do you think the Trinos, the Catu and all the other tribes will do when they find out that the Micini's Queen is weak?"

"Fight on without you?" I answered, knowing as I spoke that this was not the right answer.

"They will sell us to the Romans to save their own skins," hissed Curl. "We'd probably do the same to them," he admitted.

Looking about the camp, I could see he had a point. All around us were pots and pans, vases and vines, carts and candles and cattle. And all of this was booty, stolen from Gnaw-itch, Camulod and the many nameless villages that the army had looted. I have dabbled in the writing of history, and I have always thought that it would be unfortunate to come from a small place like a village. For no one writes about your losses. Writers of history only like to put the famous towns in their works. We have heard of the sack of the city of Tray, where the face of Helen started a bloody war, launching a thousand ships in the wrong direction. But will we hear of the battle of Lower-Chippinghamster, a three-house hamlet on the road to Camulod. Were there heroic deeds done in Chippinghamster? Was there some local beauty there, with a simple job, an eel farmer's daughter? Did she have a Kitish name, like Smellen perhaps? Will the poets write about her? Not the Roman ones at any rate. Even I will have to leave Smellen's story for the Mewids to sing about in their ballads for there is no time to write of such things. I must return to Queen's and Emperors.

I slipped into Boudicat's tent and I stood there in the gloom. The Queen's Mewid had ordered the slaves to turn the lamps down low. As I drew near, I could hardly believe it. Queen Boudicat looked awful – a pale copy of her old self. I was amazed that the poor Queen could lift a paw, but she got looked up from her bed of cushions, and told me to come closer. The warriors guarding her bed hissed, and her old Mewid glared at me and muttered.

"Sister's Daughter's husband, I am glad you are here," croaked Boudicat.

"What service can I do for you, great Queen?" I said.

"Come closer," she whispered, holding my gaze. "I believe," she began, "I mean - I know that your Roman God Clawdius has..." Her voice trailed off, as if she didn't have enough breath to get out the words.

"Put a curse on me."

"That is most unlikely," I answered.

"It is HIS work great Queen, I have seen it in Andrasta's Mirror," said a cracked voice. It was the old Mewid in the corner.

"What can mirrors show us, but a reflection of our own selves?" I said, pleased for once to have come up with an answer that was also a question. Now the Mewid would have to think of a clever answer.

"Are you sure that it is a curse great Queen?" I asked quietly, leaning close.

"Of course I'm sure!' she spat. I jumped back, thinking that a wounded Queen was probably far more dangerous than a healthy one.

"I should never have driven my chariot over your God's hollow head," said Boudicat weakly.

I looked at this once fierce warrior, and I wondered. For it was in my power to tell her that Clawdius was no god. And with the spell on of her fear broken, she might get better by herself. But something held my tongue. Would the Micini be better off without this rebel Queen to lead them into sorrow? This was one war they could not win.

"Tell me, Spartapuss. What can I do to please the Roman god Clawdius?"

"We know what will please him," said the old Mewid, "Do not worry. Everything is being prepared." Well, hearing that Mewid talk made up my mind. Whatever he had planned, I'm sure it was a long way from 'Good words, good thoughts, good deeds.' This was the way the original Mewids used to follow, before things went all sickles at midnight. I leapt across to the lamps and turned them all up, filling the tent with light.

"You are not cursed my Queen," I cried. "Clawdius was no more a god than you or I, or that old growler stirring your soup over there."

"Do not believe him great Queen," cried the old Mewid, in a rage.

"May my tongue drop out if it is not true," I said, (in the Kittish way of speaking).

"What do you know about gods, turn-tail?" hissed the old Mewid. I thought at the time that it was a good job that he didn't have his silver sickle with him, for he would have chopped me like a stalk of mistletoe.

"I know more than you about Clawdius. I worked for him once. Moments before he became the Emperor, he was hiding on top of a cupboard. I was in the room with him."

"Nonsense. He was a mighty warrior. In our songs we call him Iron Clawdius. " said the Mewid.

"The servants made that nickname up because his cushions always needed ironing," I replied. The poor Mewid had no answer for this, so I added. "And he used to pick at a spot near his collar. And he never paid his milk bill on time. Does that sound like a God to you?" Before the Mewid could answer, the Queen thanked me for coming, then told me to go.

SEPTEMBER IV

September 4th

As I write, it is raining once again. Curl has warned me to watch out. I have often thought that this was a well-meaning but foolish piece of advice. Watch out for what? News of my conversation with the Queen has spread. I may have angry Mewids on my tail. But at least the Queen is feeling better. Curl says that he was talking to the cooks. Last night, the Queen woke suddenly and ordered roast chicken, from her usual bowl.

SEPTEMBER V

September 5th

Boudicat is feeling better and ready for war. She has ordered a (great) meeting of the Micini warriors this evening. I have been invited. But I can only come to the tent after the Queen's Mewids have finished their ceremonies. Since I lit the lamps in the Queen's tent the other day, the Mewids have been avoiding me. Curl says that they curse and mutter when I pass by. I wonder what the old Mewid had in mind when he told the Queen that the Mewids know how to please the God Clawdius. I shudder to think. I bet it was not mushrooms that he had in mind

SEPTEMBER VI

September 6th

Ferulanium.

I have been put out - to walk the lonely road once again. My destination - I do not care as long as it is in the opposite direction from the unfortunate town of Ferulanium. I hear that it has been burned and flooded at the same time - which is most unusual. I will now write down the terrible events that have brought me to this ditch so that history will know the truth.

I padded into the Royal tent to find Boudicat her old self once again. It was nice to see a war-like scowl back on her face. The talking had finished, and now the Lords of the Micini were in a whirl of excitement. There were cries of "War, war, we go to war!" and the sort of shouting that warriors usually go in for.

It is said that there was a good supply of catnip in the last town that the Queen's army took. I am not good at this sort of wild partying anymore, but I did my best to join in. I shouted and leaped about as if my life depended on it - which it probably did. As the music stopped, I was thrust towards a rowdy group of warriors. Fearing another rat skinning competition, I decided to make small talk.

"So friends, you're ready to take on Governor Mewtonius at last?" I said. On hearing this, the group began to howl with laughter. I joined in the laughing too, not really knowing what I was laughing at. But suddenly, the smiles dried up. I turned to see Mane behind me. Now why this warrior decided to take against me I cannot say. I understood it no better than the nail understands the hammer. Perhaps he saw something in me that he wanted for himself? Laughter, spirit or whatever. But rather than brighten his own personality – he swore to bring me down to his grim level.

"Why are you always grinning Roman? Coming to Ferulanium? Follow behind us fighters and you'll find plenty of coins in the pockets of your dead friends. I'm sure you will have no problem sniffing them out."

I ignored this insult, so he threw me another.

"You snail-suckers could sniff out silver in a heap of rotting fish." Silence was not going to get me out of this. So I tried a question.

"Why Ferulanium? There are no Romans there." Mane did not answer. Another of the group replied.

"We've always hated the Catu – they are cursed turntails – eating scraps from out of the Roman's bowls." Then I heard myself asking.

"Is that a good reason to attack a defenseless city? Wouldn't it be better to take on Governor Mewtonius instead?"

Mane gave me a look that would have worried a wolf.

"What is it to you Roman? Do you have another house there?"

"Er, no." I replied. Mane stalked towards me and before I could move, I felt an enormous claw at my throat.

"Liar," he hissed, dragging me by my collar. Curl, who had spotted the trouble, came to my side. "Speak the truth or die."

"It is not a house, it is a field," I choked. Mane pounced, stuck out a huge paw and rubbed my face in the dirt.

"Roman land-lords!" laughed Mane. "You want to be lords all right – with the land of our ancestors. What do you think of your friend now, Curl?"

Struggling up from the dust, I heard a familiar voice.

"Is it true?" demanded Curl.

"Well, I used to be a land owner," I began. "I have done pretty well out of the comb business. But now I have lost my Gnaw-itch Nest egg, my Camulod Cottage and my Londump loft. Now, I fear that my field in Ferulanium will go the same way. It is a terrible worry!"

Curl flashed me a look, turned his back on me and stalked off without another word.

"Don't fret, money-grubber!" hissed Mane. "I will take that worry away for you." Now, this is exactly the sort of thing that I had feared since he first set eyes on me. The crowd began to jeer and clap, apart from the ones who had been on the catnip, who just wobbled.

"You say you were once a gladiator, so we will fight Roman style." Not knowing what to say I mumbled.

"That is a good idea. But it is a shame that we do not have an arena."

"There's one in Ferulanium," cried an excited voice.

"Thank you friend," I replied, shivering slightly.

"It's a bit small though," said one of the pot-washers.

"It'll be big enough for me to put an end to this bag of offal!" laughed Mane. "Make peace with your gods, for tomorrow you'll squeak when I skewer you with this, Roman pig."

BATTLE FIELD

So the next day I stepped into the Arena at Ferulanium to face the Great Warrior Mane. It was one of my longer fights but I soon remembered my gladiator training. The old moves came back to me, and I send the villain running from the Arena with a walnut sized bump on his thick head and his tail between his legs.

Ah, dear reader, if only Fortune had spun it thus, but it was not to be. For one thing, Mane's tail is as thick as a Purrmanian sausage, and it would not fit easily between his legs. In truth, that night I could think of nothing but the terrors of a bloody fight and Mane's promise to do a number of things to me which I will not now write down. I did not give up at first. I did try to remember my training, but I am too old for leaping around now. The floors of these tents are hard. I would say that it is impossible to pitch your tent in this land without finding stones beneath your sleeping place. Cushions to practice your rolling are in short supply. Also, chicken was on the menu that night. So you could say that the maggot of fear ate into the apple of my courage. Well, my courage is more of pea than an apple, but seeing as there are no worm-like creatures that feast on peas - perhaps I should leave that picture in my pen. In short, I did not wait for morning for a test of my courage against Mane in the arena. Instead, I slipped from my tent in the early light. When I was sure that no one was following me, I ran like a hunting dog, from Mane and his skewer.

Pole of Honour

As I fled, I thought about honour. For where is the honour in Mane, who has a chest that you could store salt-fish in, fighting an old bag of bones like me? I am no spring-chicken. In fact, I'd struggle to catch a spring chicken - even one with broken wings. Why should the weak and the strong have the same 'honour'? I would say that I have some honour, but not enough to get me speared on a sharp pole. Especially as the whole row is over my field. This is likely to be flooded when the Queen's attackers dam the river. At least the mud should be safe under water. I hope it will not wash away as it is a valuable local building material. In fact the builder who sold me the field said that it was most rich in this material. He said I would struggle to find a field this muddy in all the land of the Kitons.

CURL FRIEND

I have left without saying farewell to Queen Boudicat. She will not need my help to attack and wreck a town of innocents. And I am quite sure she can lose the next battle against Governor Mewtonius without me. However, there is one thing that is worrying me. I fear for poor Curl. Although he stalked off the other day, it was understandable. I did not know that the lands of his family, that he had lost to the money-lenders, are in Ferulanium, where I have bought my field. I do worry about him. I would not want him to be there when the Governor catches up with Queen Boudicat.

As I padded out of camp, the whiskers on my right side gave a terrible twinge, and I could smell something on the wind. At first I thought that it was last night's goose pie gone rotten. But soon, I recognised the smell. It was a scent that had first struck my nose back in the Queen's (great) Hall as I swung above that terrible pit. It is not the sort of smell that is easy to forget. The unfortunate smell of horse and boar together. It is an unnatural combination that I hope I will never have to sniff again in all of my days. I fear that the Mewids may have some mischief up their sleeeves. And they have very long sleeves on those nasty white gowns of theirs. Long enough to hide a silver sickle, or worse.

September XV

September 15th

The House I Left Behind

Well, here I am at last at my dear Matling Street Mansionette. It is rather quiet, and I have seen no sign of the housekeeper who we pay to keep the place ready for us. That is probably for the best, as she may ask for coin and my pockets are nearly empty. I am a town cat, and not used to the ways of the simple county folk here in the far north of this land. I passed a gamekeeper and his wife on the way up Matling Street. They were from the Catre tribe, by the look of their ginger coats. He was carrying a tasty looking chicken. Now Matling Street is the only proper road about these parts and I have not seen a soul about. The whole country seems empty. As food is scarce, I decided to see if I could buy myself a chicken dinner, so I hailed him with a friendly wave of the paw. I know a little of the Catre's language that they speak around these parts. So I spoke very slowly in the local tongue.

"Well met, friend! Your bird looks tasty," I said. The old Catre made no answer. He just gave me a strange look and continued on his way, faster than before. By now I was hungry and a chicken was just what I needed. So I tried again, this time far louder but keeping my sentences very short and slow. For I remembered that my friend Cursus once told me that this is the only way to make someone understand you in a foreign language.

"You! You have bird. Very tasty! How much you want?" And to show that I was in earnest, I got my last coin out and waved it in his face. I was surprised when his wife grabbed the chicken and began to hit me about the face with it causing a feather to stick up my nose. Running off, I had a horrible feeling that the fellow may have thought that I wanted to buy his wife. Although given the state of her coat I would have said that a silver coin was a good offer.

When I arrived in my house I remembered that we have an enormous sausage, imported from Purrmania in the larder. It was so big that we had to hire a cart to bring it from the merchant. There is also a good supply of dried cod fish, and there is no shortage of water as it falls from the sky around here. I am now getting ready for a quiet life in the countryside. I must stay here for a month at least before returning to Londump to meet my wife. She may not like the idea of country living, but she and my son will have to get used to it as all our other homes have been destroyed by war, fire and flood. There must be a thousand good reasons for trading the bustle of the dirty town for a new life of here in the Kittish countryside. I have decided to make a long list for my wife, in order to convince her.

SEPTEMBER XVI

September 16th

Country Life

My list is not going very well. I have not got beyond fresh air and a plentiful supply of field mice. I suppose I have many reasons to be happy, although when your life is not in danger, the small things become more important. Some villain has taken my Überbanger. The enormous sausage disappeared from the larder last night. I have made an offering to the household gods - who may tell me who the thief is. There is still no sign of my housekeeper, who has a key. As well as the missing Überbanger, some of the scraps from last night have gone. I have been cold as a codfish today, as it has not stopped raining since I arrived. I cannot get the underfloor heating to work, no matter how many times I try to light it.

But this is the least of my troubles. Last night, I was surprised to see a crowd straggling up Matling St towards the woods. We bought this house for a very good price. My wife complained that it was too close to the road. Perhaps she was right about this, as she is about most things except cooking.

I decided to put out the lights and shut up the windows. Still, at least I have the front garden, which would be a beautiful place to sit if the rain stops.

September XVII

September 17th

The Battle of Matling St

When the historians of the Feline Empire write of the battle of Matling St, there is one detail that they are not likely to remember. Matling St is but tentails length from my house. That is why I, Spartapuss can tell all that happened on that dark day in the history of this bleak and soaking land. Every night this week I woke up to noises on the street outside. I peaked out to see a trickle of lights - as the travellers made their way past my house. The trouble with a trickle is that it can soon become a stream. And so it was with this. I spent hours picking their rubbish out of my front garden, and chasing them away from my water feature. This does not contain any fish. I put up a sign to point this out, but I doubt that the locals can read catin. By the third day, I began to see banners that I recognised. The blue claw flags of the Micini. It seems that the followers of Queen Boudicat had somehow got in front of her army. Well, I was picking the fish hooks out of my pool again when I heard a 'thwoccking' noise and felt a rush of wind past my face. There were cries and shouts from the road: "It is starting!" and "They are raining hell upon us." And so it was that Governor Mewtonius had got a big force together up behind the hill. The battle was not starting, in fact he was trying out his catapults and stone-throwing machines before the battle. The Governor always has a go himself. He cannot resist a ballista, it is said.

I cowered to the ground and looked up to see the sky thick with missiles coming at me - like flies towards a dropped kebab. Fortune must have spun me a good one - for most of the stones flew too far and sailed right over my roof. Except one - which crashed into my wife's apple tree - splitting it from root to tip. I was not sad to see this sight, as there is a most annoying blackbird that sits in this tree and keeps me awake all night. I decided at once to run - not wanting to be caught up in the battle that was to come.

So I packed a few things - some biscuits and some dried-cod. With a great effort of will, I gave up on the idea of finding the Überbanger. I was wondering whether it is worth locking the gates of a mansionette that is about to be flattened by falling stones, when I saw a Micini warrior charging down the hill towards me. He had a most fierce look. He was blue from head to tail from wode, and waving furiously. My heart stopped for an instant. I feared that it was Mane, come to carry out his threats. However, I soon saw that the runner was smaller than Mane and not carrying a skewer large enough for that purpose. When he reached my wall, I helped him over - and we were both nearly ground to dust by a stone the size of a flour sack.

"Curl, old friend," I purred, pleased to see him again. Then I had a thought and added. "If it is about the challenge – you can tell Mane to pick on something his own size. One of those rocks perhaps? My fighting days are over."

Now Curl, who had just been running for his very life, was breathing so hard that the air seemed to tear in and out of his mouth.

"I bring a message, from the Queen," he said at last. "She bids you come and join the victory!"

"And what if I do not want to join?" I asked.

"She has thought of that," said Curl. "If it goes badly for us, and we do not win, you are to see that the Mewids get this."

He threw me a small leather bag. On opening it, I found an enormous silver torc. I recognised it at once as the one that Queen Boudicat had been wearing the first time I saw her. I was amazed to see how brightly the silver gleamed, even on a dark day such as this.

"Don't worry Spartapud," said Curl. "I'll be back for it tomorrow. Our fighters are ready. And see, we outnumber the Romans ten to one! How can we lose?"

"Curl," I said, shaking my head, "I would not be so sure. Roman legions have fought bigger armies than the Queens before, and won."

Curl laughed. "See you back here tomorrow!"

"And what of the Queen? What will she do if you

lose the day?" I asked.

"The Romans will not take her alive," said Curl, pulling at his collar. "If we lose, which we won't, she'll be laughing from Summerlands."

"You mean she is going to take her own life?" I said in amazement.

"We all are," said Curl matter-of-factly. "It is decided. In death we will have a great victory."

Curl stroked his collar. I saw a tiny piece of glass, like a little barrel. I guessed that this contained poison, brewed by the Mewids. I could not believe that he was sitting there, smiling as he told me of this plan. Now something stirred within me, maybe it was the god Paws - for I suddenly felt a heat flowing up through my spine and deep into my old bones. At first I thought it was the spicy sauce on the kebab I'd had at breakfast. Then I knew it to be anger!

"Oh yes," I hissed. "What a 'great' victory, It's a shame that none of you will be alive to celebrate it!"

"It will be a victory nevertheless. The Mewids have promised it," said Curl, surprised to see me like this. Well, I can hardly believe what I did next. For I picked up a torch and I lit it quickly. Then I threw open the door of my last house. I had spent the last weeks bravely fighting against the destruction of my homes, but now I was sick of the fight. It was time to surrender and have done with it.

"Watch and learn!" I hissed, bristling with rage. I sprang into my house and set light to everything that might burn. Then leaping back to the door, I cast the torch into the centre of the fire. Soon the room began to fill with sparks. The timbers crackled as the flames embraced them and held them tight. Great billows of black smoke blew from the room, stinging my eyes.

"There," I said, with salt tears running down. "I have burned down my home – so that no one - Roman or Kiton - can take it from me." I threw myself into a puddle. "Here I sit, in the mud. What a wonderful victory I have won. I shall celebrate tonight when I lay my head on the cold road for a pillow." And with that, the rain began to fall. Curl padded over.

"Get up," he said. "Maybe we can change her mind."

As we made our way up my path, he suddenly stopped and sniffed the smokey air.

"What is it?" I said, fearing that he might have changed his mind.

"Can you smell burning sausage?" he asked.

CRUSH COURSE

As we ran up the hill, my last house burnt behind me. It was no time for looking back, as the stones from the Roman machines were still falling. I was surprised that the ballistas had not found their range yet. I later learned that the XIV Legion were in charge of stone throwing - and they are known as the worst shots in the Empire. When the mad Emperor Catligula declared war on the sea and ordered his troops to stand on the

121

beach and fire, they are said to have missed the water. Missiles tore the air as Curl and I puffed up that muddy slope. At the top of the hill we saw a sight that would have sent Paws the war-god slinking back to his basket. I could see no Romans, only a great mass of Kitons. Not just Micini but Catres, Trinos and who knows what other tribes - massed in a great crowd before us. This was the 'great army' that Curl had boasted about. There were so many - standing like poppies in a field. And already they were taking a pounding from rocks and flaming spears flung down from on high.

"Where are the Romans?" I asked. For so big was the Kiton army, that from where we were standing at the back, we could not get a sight of the Roman attackers. Curl pointed to the left where the ground closed into a narrow gorge with steep sides. The Romans had their stone-throwing machines set up on the slopes of both sides of this gorge.

It was not good for the Kitons. For although Boudicat's army was huge, Governor Mewtonius had out foxed the Queen. For if her battle chariots charged through that narrow space, there would be no advantage in greater numbers. The crush would work to Rome's favour. I thought of what would happen to the proud Micini army, if they ran into that narrow trap. They would be cut down like corn at harvest time. The very thought of it made me shudder.

HOT DOGS

"Fish-plates - fresh today," called a friendly voice. Here at the back of the great Kiton army, the food sellers were hard at work. Taking my chance, I bought a bag of salted-cod and some roasted chicken pieces. I could see some of the families had brought their young ones up in carts, to the very edge of the battle. A pair of small white lap-dogs had got loose and were running about madly, excited at the smell of the roast chicken.

"Got any eels left?" asked Curl, but before he could agree a price, a great stone came flying towards us and sent the crowds scattering in panic. I searched in vain for Curl, but he was gone. In the crush, it was impossible to find him. After a while, I wondered which way to move, for move I must. I asked the Goddess Fortune, and I thought she said "Go left!" Carefully, I threaded my way through that crowd. Now it was not easy to move to the left, for crowds have their own flow, like rivers, and much of the time I was pushing against this. No matter how I tried to make my own way I was being forced to go with the rest. Twice I fell, and was almost trampled in the fray. For you do not look where you walk in a crowd. Then I heard terrible shouts and cries to the Goddess Andrasta, Woool Almighty and the Great Mother to save them. When I made the far edge of the crowd, my heart nearly stopped. There were the fighters of the glorious XXth Legion - trampling the fallen warriors with their iron-shod claws. There was a great cry from the Micini side as they stood whisker to whisker with their enemy for the first time.

CRUSHED GINGER

"In Peus name, this is it," I thought, gazing at the legions as they earned their biscuits. Ever closer we were pushed, towards the stabbing line of Romans. I was afraid and I cried out. I cannot now report what it was that I said, but I think it may be a phrase that I picked up a sailor I once knew. My paws wobbled and went weak beneath me. In fact it was not just my paws. All of me felt weak, from my grey whiskers to the tip of my tail. I wondered what madness had brought me to this sorry end. I am no warrior, like the great Hercatules. I am just an old ginger who has done rather nicely by selling silver brushes to a land where they fear the bath more than the battlefield. You are too old for this, but too young to die, I thought. It was useless. For I had no weapon. Even if I had wanted to fight, the crush was so thick that it was impossible. The proud Kitons could not even raise their beloved broadswords, never mind swing them at anything.

SWEET CHARIOT

At last I heard a shout. The line of Romans broke before me and scattered like seed on the wind. I felt myself being lifted up and carried forward, with the force of a breaking wave. When I opened my eyes, I saw her face. Her amber eyes scanned the lines for her next target. He thick coat was blue with wode. Queen Boudicat had got the Lords of the Micini together and ridden down a sheer slope for one last chariot charge.

"Great Queen! Thank you!" I cried.

"Greetings, Sister's daughter's husband. What brings you here?" Boudicat smiled, as if we'd met over the fish-course at a friend's birthday party, rather than in the thick of battle.

"I came because I thought. I mean, I believed that you were going to..."

"Take my own life?" smiled Boudicat. "I will have some of theirs first." With that, she pulled an arrow from her quiver and in one smooth movement let it fly. As the dart found its target, she called to her dogs to come about. The chariot came round in an arc and soon we were flying back along the Roman lines. The Romans stood like statues - as if Paws himself had got their tongues. At last, a fat Scenturian broke out from the Roman line. When his chance came, he took it. Ducking a spear-thrust, he sprung out in front of us, leapt across the backs of the dogs and clawed his way up. I shivered as I saw the long knife between his teeth. He was so close that I could see that the blade was chipped and the handle was filthy. I tutted on seeing this - as our legions are only allowed to use their proper weapons and not pick up any old thing they find on the battle field. It is set down in the

Sprei Militari - our Roman rules of war.

"Where is your gladius Scenturian?" I shouted, wanting to shame him for not having a proper sword, which used to be a serious offence in the old days. "What in Peus name do you think you're doing with that dirty old knife?" I called

"This!" he spat, going for the Queen's throat. Yet Boudicat had feinted to the right, and the blade found nothing but thin air. Before the fat one could get a second blow in, I let out a cry and clawed at him with all the strength that I had left. This cannot have been a large amount, for I watched his nose puff in as my claw hit and then pop back out again, only slightly redder than it had been before.

"My old mum can hit harder than that," he laughed. On hearing that insult, I decided to hit him with everything I had. The first thing I could find was a bag of salted cod pieces, that I had been saving for later. It was well salted, and he lost his grip for a moment, as he felt the sting of the salt in his eyes. But it was no use, for he pulled himself back up with his other paw and took that horrible knife from between his teeth again.

"You fight like a small female," he hissed.

"Let's see if you can die like a warrior," hissed Boudicat. With a cry to her dogs and she made an expert turn and pitched the chariot onto one wheel. It span around in an arc, leaving our fat Scenturian friend snagged on a small tree.

WRONG BOW

"Nice work great Queen," I shouted. But before the words were leaving my mouth the left dog lost its footing in a ditch and our wheel snagged on a rock. The whole rig flew up in the air, dogs and all and turned over. When I opened my eyes, I found myself in the middle of chaos. By the time I had managed to wriggle free, the dogs had ran off howling as we had landed in a patch of fire. At last I found the Queen, trapped under a wheel. Her back leg was crumpled. She did not cry out - but said calmly,

"Give me my bow of gold."

"I'm afraid it's burning," I said. "But I've got some arrows if you desire?"

Boudicat strung an arrow to her bow and took aim at the Roman line. But with her back leg hurt, she did not have the strength to pull it back properly and she slumped back down into the wreckage. I took her by the paw and helped her up.

"Here," I said, passing her a spear to use as a crutch. Just then, a volley of arrows smacked into the tree behind us. I shivered as I saw their shafts quivering, their points set deep in the wood.

"Take cover!" I cried, diving into a bush. I looked up to see Boudicat, take the spear from under her arm and hurl it at the Romans. Crash followed cry as the archer fell from his hiding place. Without her crutch, the Queen wobbled.

"What will you fight with now?" I asked.

"These will do," she answered – extending her claws. I was wondering how to reason with a warrior Queen when all of the sudden I heard a noise which was quite unexpected. It was lost for a moment - and then I heard it again - the unmistakable sound of yapping. It was the two little white dogs that I had seen earlier. Here they were, chasing each other and play fighting in the wreck and smoke of a battlefield.

"Hail friends!" I cried. "You two look as fit as a pair of marsh-fleas." "We like to exercise," smiled the first. And to prove his point he leapt high in the air and grabbed a branch from one of the few trees that was still standing.

"Ever pulled a chariot?" I asked.

"No!" yapped his brother. "And we're not about to start now," said the first.

"That's a pity," I said, pulled out the bag of roasted chicken wings.

"I thought you might like to help us, and get a taste of some Royal food, as a reward."

"Royal food!" said the first dog, leaping up on his back legs and giving out a yelp.

"What is it?" said his brother, sniffing the bag frantically.

"Only dragon wings," I said. "The Queen eats them all day long." I threw a small piece to each of them - and their tails began to wag.

"Delicious," yapped the first.

"Tastes like chicken," said his brother.

"Are you sure you won't help? There's plenty more where that came from," I asked.

"Live and learn is what I say," said the first dog, licking his lips.

"You're never too old for new tricks," said the second. Now getting them into the harness was a struggle - due to their small size. These two dogs were small - but they were amazingly strong for their size. With care, we managed to haul the turned chariot up onto its wheels again. At last I helped the Queen into her place.

"Where too?" came a shout from the dogs.

"To battle!" cried Boudicat. The dogs were not too pleased with this, and refused to move another step.

"Move!" hissed the Queen. "Onwards to battle and death!"

"Do you mind if we go the long way?" I asked. For I remembered that Curl said the Lords of the Micini were camped in a spot under the cliff in the woods.

MINE CAMP

Well, I was so relieved to see the Micini camp that I threw the whole bag of dragon's wings to the dog team. Boudicat was welcomed by the Lords of the Micini and helped into her tent. I went to follow behind her, but my path was blocked by a familiar figure in a white robe.

"The Queen's tent is no place for an unbeliever," he said. Too tired to argue, I threw myself down on a patch of grass outside, and decided to wait. I did not have long to wait, for the next face to come out of that tent was a familiar one. It was Mane. He was blooded and bruised but he did not seem battle weary. On seeing the royal chariot he let out a great hiss.

"Where are the Queen's dogs?" he cried. Now I must admit that the two lap dogs must have looked like an odd sight - as they were only one third the size of a usual chariot dog. Their white coats did not help. And their tongues were unusually long, and blue in colour.

"Who is responsible for this disgrace?" spat Mane, lumbering towards me. I did not know what to do. I had no strength left in my body to run. My mind span, as I searched for an excuse. But it did not matter, for before I could answer - Mane took hold of me and dragged me to the foot of the cliff. He hauled me over a grey rock, to a ledge. I could not take my eyes off the gaping mouth of the mineshaft, which dropped down to unknown depths.

"Wait! I can explain." I cried. But it was no use. Mane lifted me up and cast me down the mineshaft. As I fell, I thought my life's thread coming to its end. To my amazement, I soon stopped falling and began to slide. I clawed madly at the rock and finally came to a rest, although the ground beneath me did not feel solid. The hole was dark as a tomb. I should know, for I have been in a couple of tombs. And I can honestly say that the smell down here was worse.

THE LONG DARK

Now I could not make out anything in the gloom, so I clawed at the walls to try to give shape to the long darkness around me. The walls were sheer rock but the floor beneath was wooden, made of thin slats and beams. I did not know it at the time, but I was standing on the roof of an enormous cage. The Mewids had lowered it down into the shaft with ropes. Looking up, I could just make out the light at the top of the shaft. And into this point of light stepped a figure, all in white.

"There's been a mistake. Could you fetch a ladder?" I called. I felt something land nearby. It was sharp to the touch. I later learned that it was a crown made of apple branches.

"There is no mistake. Get ready for your end," called the Mewid above me. "Many must give themselves. This is the only way to beat the Romans."

The Catre tribe have an old saying, that there is no point arguing with a Mewid. So, for once I did not waste my breath. Besides, my nose was full of a smell of the mine, both terrible and familiar. It was a foul stench, half pig, half horse. I scanned the shadows behind me for movements, but all was still. Finally, I looked upwards to the light again and saw a second shape appear behind my sickle-waiving friend.

"Mane!" I called. "Mane, are you there?" "It is a pity that the Goddess Andrasta will see that the great

Mane, noble warrior of the Micini, does not have the stomach for a fight."

"The Queen has forbidden it," he roared. I smiled, for I had a feeling that he would not be able to resist.

"Mane, you sack of dirt. I challenge you, come down and fight me claw to claw, if you dare."

Well, I looked up and wondered. But I did not have long to wait. There was a shout of rage followed by a scuffling noise and a great crash. The floor shook and fell away, and I was left clinging to the bare rock by my claws.

Mane, it seemed, was a fool. And a big one at that. Big enough to jump down the mine-shaft, crash through the roof I was standing on and fall into the creature's cage below. There was a horrible snorting noise and then a grunting roar, and the rest was silence.

The idea had been to get Mane to climb down on a rope or ladder. I never expected him to leap into the abyss. So my main problem was gone, but it had taken the floor away with it. In a panic, I tried to get a better hold of the rock wall but the rock was weak and crumbled away to the touch. I could not hold myself for long. There was no way to climb back out. The beast's pit was darker than my wife's best stew (when she follows the recipe). I was stuck like a burnt dumpling at the bottom of the pan. If I dropped down I might be able to run off into the darkness, but would the creature follow? Was there a way out of these caves?

CRUSHING BOAR

I will never know the answer. For I heard a snort. Then I felt a terrible shaking of the bars where I was standing. I thought of one good practical piece of advice to tell my son. "If your life is in danger, and you hold a conversation with yourself to try to decide what to do, make it a short one, and make sure that you do not speak out loud!" The bars shuddered, shaken by a blow from an enormous hoof or tusk. I slipped and followed Mane, down to the floor of the pit where the creature was waiting.

I landed in a puddle of slime, or worse. Immediately, I searched my pockets for the one thing that might save me - an apple. But Fortune spun me a wrong one, as I thrown it at the Romans earlier in the day. How I wish I had listened to the words of my dear mother, when she said that "Apples are for eating, not throwing."

I was not long before I heard a roar behind me. Then I was hit. It could not have been full force, for the Boar Horse's tusks could pull up oak trees. I was alive still. I was tossed across the cave with the sort of care that a school pupil takes when he throws off his sandals. I tried not to cry out, as the Boar Horse hunts by sound and smell. I am surprised that it can smell anything at all, except its own foul stench. But I shifted my weight towards my right paw and a sharp pain forced me to cry out. I thought that my foot must be broken. I tried to move, but the creature came close. So close that I could feel its breath. I shivered as I remembered Curl's warning – its bite was death. That is if it doesn't trample you to death before biting you. I began to shiver and tremble. I have always had a terrible fear of being eaten. I would certainly not want to be eaten by an animal that should be grazing in a field or snuffling for roots in the forest.

Just then my eyes were burned by an orange light. I thought it might have been in Summerlands, as the Kitons call the world beyond. But shortly afterwards I knew the light was coming from a burning torch that had been thrown down the shaft. In the flickering torchlight, I came nose-to-nose with a shocking sight. For the Boar Horse is the most unfortunate, most misshapen beast that I have ever seen. Even its own mother would choke at the sight of its matted mane and turn away from that tangle of tusks. The bristles weren't helping either. I have since made an offering to Fleanus, the Goddess of Beauty and Grooming, that the Gods might smash its mould. No creature that unpleasant should walk this earth. Not in the daylight anyway. Face-to-face with it, I did not wonder that the silversmiths decided to put a side view of the animal on the Micini's coins. Who would want to carry a picture like that around in their pocket?

Now whether by nature, or through long years of living in its pit, the creature both feared and hated the light. It roared and reared towards me, but backed away from the flickering torch. Twice I was almost crushed by its great tusks, which grazed the cave walls sending stone chips flying. It is a shame I did not have a bucket, as it is said there is a good market for stone chips in Ferulanium, on account of the flooding.

At last, Fortune span me a bad one, for the torch flame began to die in the thin air of the pit. At last the creature had me trapped. It gave a snort, ripping grooves in the ground with its great front hooves. Then sprang. Yet in mid-leap, it changed direction and lunged away from me, towards the other side of the shaft. Then it fell to ground, useless as a split gourd. A good few minutes later, I got up the courage to draw nearer. In the gathering darkness, I wondered what magic could stop such a creature in mid leap? But it was not the work of the gods. There in its throat I saw the reason why it fell. A golden arrow was stuck in the thing's throat. Crushed beneath the beast was Boudicat herself. If not the cleverest queen that the Land of the Kitons has ever known, she was surely the bravest. Around her neck, the little poison barrel was empty. The venom was not in the Queen's belly, it was on her arrow tip. On her face she wore a scowl, and her paw still held her golden bow, ready to string up one last shot. Even bitten to death, she did not know when she was beaten.

SEPTEMBER XXIX

September 29th

As I write, I sit at the dock side with a bag of gold in my pocket. The rain falls in grey sheets. I doubt that the fish can feel it. I was in no mood for a meeting with the Mewids, so I sold Queen's silver torc for a pretty sum. I will need this money to buy a gift when I tell my wife about the destruction of our three houses and the flooding of our field.

I have decided to meet them in Rome. Perhaps ill news will feel better in the sunshine. And what of the Micini? I fear the news is no better for that tribe. I have not seen poor Curl since the day of the battle. I went back to my ruined house and waited for him, but he never came. Whether he is taken, or escaped to Maul, I cannot say. That day at Matling Street belonged to Rome. For their crushing and stamping, the XXth legion won the title 'The Victorious XXth' and a year's supply of eels. The XIVth legion just got the eels, even though they were victorious too. The Emperor got his claws into the Mewids and the tax collector got his taxes. The tribes that rose up were put back down. The tribes that had not joined Boudicat's war got rewarded. Their Kings were made citizens of Rome. History will record that Queen Boudicat drank deadly poison – rather than live under the rule of the Romans. But that is just history, not her story.

A NOTE FROM THE AUTHOR

'Some readers may be wondering what happened to Furg, (the young Micini cat that Spartapuss went to look for at the end of *Die Clawdius*). *Boudicat* is set some eighteen years after the Invasion, and after some research, I decided that this amazing warrior queen deserved her own book. I plan to return to the story of Furg later in the Spartapuss series.'

Books in The Spartapuss Series:

I Am Spartapuss (Book I)
Catligula (Book II)
Die Clawdius (Book III)
Boudicat (Book IV)

Spartapuss will return in *Spartapuss Rex*

www.mogzilla.co.uk

I AM SPARTAPUSS

By Robin Price

In the first adventure in the Spartapuss series...
Rome AD 36. The mighty Feline Empire rules the world.
Spartapuss, a ginger cat is comfortable managing Rome's
finest Bath and Spa. But Fortune has other plans for him.
Spartapuss is arrested and imprisoned by Catligula, the
Emperor's heir. Sent to a school for gladiators, he must
fight and win his freedom in the Arena - before his oppo-
nents make dog food out of him.

'This witty Roman romp is history with cattitude.'
Junior Magazine (Scholastic)

ISBN 10: 09546576-0-8
ISBN 13: 978-0-9546576-0-4

UK £6.99
USA $14.95/ CAN $16.95

For USA/ Canada orders contact:
Independent Publishers Group
Phone: 312.337.0747
FAX: 312.337.5985
http://www.ipgbook.com/

Download free Spartapuss wallpaper at
www.mogzilla.co.uk

CATLIGULA

By Robin Price

Was this the most unkindest kit of all?

In the second adventure in the Spartapuss series...

Catligula becomes Emperor and his madness brings Rome to within a whisker of disaster. When Spartapuss gets a job at the Imperial Palace, Catligula wants him as his new best friend. The Spraetorian Guard hatch a plot to destroy this power-crazed puss in an Arena ambush. Will Spartapuss go through with it, or will our six-clawed hero become history?

ISBN 978-0-9546576-1-1

UK £6.99
USA $10.95/ CAN $14.95

For USA/ Canada orders contact:
Independent Publishers Group
Phone: 312.337.0747
FAX: 312.337.5985
http://www.ipgbook.com/

Download free Spartapuss wallpaper at www.mogzilla.co.uk

DIE CLAWDIUS

By Robin Price

'You will die, Clawdius!'

In third adventure in the Spartapuss series...

Clawdius, the least likely Emperor in Roman history, needs to show his enemies who's boss. So he decides to invade Spartapuss' home – The Land of the Kitons.
As battle lines are drawn, Spartapuss must take sides.
Can the magic of the Mewids help him to make the right choice?

'Another fantastic story in this brilliantly inventive series. Any reader (young and old) will enjoy these books!'
Teaching and Learning Magazine

ISBN 978-095-46576-8-0

UK £6.99   USA $10.95/ CAN $14.95

For USA/ Canada orders contact:
Independent Publishers Group
Phone: 312.337.0747
FAX: 312.337.5985
http://www.ipgbook.com/